THE HISTORY OF VEGAS

THE HISTORY OF VEGAS

Stories

Jodi Angel

CHRONICLE BOOKS
SAN FRANCISCO

This is a work of fiction. Names, places, characters, and incidents are products of the author's imagination or are used fictionally. Any resemblance to actual people, places, or events is entirely coincidental.

Library of Congress Cataloging-in-Publication Data available.

ISBN 0-8118-4625-3

Manufactured in the United States of America

Designed by Celery Design Collaborative

Jacket designed by Celery Design Collaborative and Ayako Akazawa

Distributed in Canada by Raincoast Books

9050 Shaughnessy Street

Vancouver, British Columbia V6P 6E5

10 9 8 7 6 5 4 3 2 1

Chronicle Books LLC

85 Second Street

San Francisco, California 94105

www.chroniclebooks.com

To Pam, Jack, and Jay for not only opening
the doors, but for finding them for me.
To my mom and Scott for being unconditional.

And most of all, to Carolyn and Shelby, with love.

CONTENTS

THE HISTORY OF VEGAS

PORTIONS

Tim kept calling it dirt weed and I couldn't stop laughing. I tried to finger-comb my hair when I laughed so that it fell dark and sunlit over my shoulders and one of the guys might notice, but then I saw myself trying to work my hair just right, and that seemed funnier than dirt weed and Tim. We were smoking stems and shake down by the river and burning time on a Wednesday. We should've been in school—all of us—Tim and Rich and me and Dusty, but it was April, two months from graduation, and we didn't care anymore. Dusty had her head in my lap and I couldn't stop touching her face. Her sister worked at a salon and Dusty's eyebrows were waxed into a clean line. I wanted to run my finger over them. Tim rolled up his jeans and waded out into the fake surf of the river where there was enough of a foam line to make it seem as though the river carried more than the sifted scales of dead fish and the runoff of winter storms. He stopped before his feet got wet and he threw a flat rock across the surface so that it bunny-hopped the wake and then sank fifty yards from the shore. "Your sister got a boyfriend yet?" Rich asked me, and the rock Tim was skipping jumped twice, rebounded, and disappeared from the surface.

"That shit ain't funny," Tim said, and Dusty sat up and left my lap to take the brunt of the north wind that had picked up in the last half hour.

The beach point was empty in April, but there were the sloughed-off remains of fishermen—nightcrawler containers, knots of tight blue line, catfish bait bags. I wondered what it might be like to come out on this bank and fish, sit with my ass balanced on some rocks and wait for a steelhead to arc the pole. It would probably be boring without dope, without Rich and Tim and Dusty, without the jettisoned remains of our ice chest winking thin sunlight off aluminum.

"I have to get going," I said, and Tim waded out farther in the water, out beyond his bare legs, until the edge of his jeans darkened in the doughnut beneath his knees. When he stepped out of the water his legs were pink with cold. I thought about telling him that his legs were salmon pink, but my high was almost gone, and even though my observation sounded funny to me, I knew that by the time I said it out loud, it wouldn't be funny anymore.

Rich gathered up the spent cans and Dusty reset her ponytail. Tim slipped on his Chucks and we all stood around for a minute and listened to the river. I liked the smell of wet weeds and algae. The river was like white noise on a television station without reception. The river was the kind of noise that I could fall asleep to at night.

"I thought your mom doesn't get home until after six," Dusty said. She had already found a rough stone to use as an emery board and she was filing her nails while we stood around and stared out at the water.

"She gets home whenever," I said, "but I have to be home for Jess." I was six years older than Jessica. My birth had been planned and Jess had come along like an afterthought. When I was in first grade I brought her for show-and-tell like a hamster, and my parents had let me raise her ever since.

"What I don't get is why you're baby-sitting her, Samantha," Rich said. "I mean, when I was in fuckin' junior high, I went home and nobody sat there with me."

"My mom works late. It's too much time to spend alone," I said.

Rich had his hand cupped over his mouth and I could tell he was choking back something he wanted to say.

"What?" I said.

Rich turned his face away and the river took the sound. "Forget him," Dusty said, "he's just being an asshole."

I brushed the dirt off of my feet and pulled my socks on. Jess had been in charge of the laundry for the past two weeks and all of my white socks were now a weak shade of blue.

"Just say it, fuckwad," I said to Rich. I had slept with him. I didn't mean to, but Tim had been grounded and Dusty was in Pittsburgh visiting her grandma. Rich had his dad's truck and a twelve-pack of Pabst. We went to the park and sat at the curb with the engine ticking and the radio playing oldies. He kept telling jokes about elephants. I finally just put my lips over his mouth and gapped my kiss wide enough to take his tongue because I knew it was what he wanted, knew it was why he called me, knew why the streetlights buzzed over our heads and the beer was free. I let him sink it into me right there on the vinyl seat of his dad's truck, let him leave the rubber rolled tight as chewing gum on the floorboards, let him put the come-thrust deep and leave it there while his mouth tried to catch up with the rest of his body.

"I gotta get home," I said again, and this time Rich started walking and Dusty took my hand and Tim carried the garbage out from the rock banks alone.

In the parking lot Tim waited until Dusty was in the car next to Rich and the tailpipe was kicking fumes. Tim's car was on blocks in his parents' garage with the engine gutted like a three-point buck. I was his ride and he had the senior prom corsage in his refrigerator to prove it. "Can you drop me at my place?" he asked. Rich lived less than a mile from Tim's house, same side of the street in another shit brown house, but Tim knew if I was running late, I'd sooner give a blow job than fend off fucking and leave Jess sitting on the front steps alone.

I drove Tim home in silence and when my tires met the gravel of his driveway he slid next to me and rubbed his hand on my thigh. He found a station on the radio and let his head fall back against the bench seat. I kept the engine running while the dogs barked behind the fence until I sat up in my seat again.

The steps were empty and the house was quiet when I got home. The sunset was buried in thick dark clouds and there was the cheap lilac of false twilight feathered across the sky. The answering machine was flashing and I knew it was the attendance office calling to inform my mom that I hadn't been in school today. I erased a hang-up, the notice that I was absent again, a telemarketer who wanted my mom to call and claim her free gift, and the main office at Jess's school. "Hello . . . Jess needs to be picked up by a parent or guardian . . ." The voice sounded fat and depressed. The message paused and cut off with a click. I called the real-estate office where my mom worked—Ben Bailey Realty—and I listened to a machine pick up, an automated voice direct me to hold, and the Bee Gees singing "Don't throw it all away, our love" to organ music. The secretary took the line and I asked for my mother. The phone beeped twice and then my mother answered. She sounded like her shirt was unbuttoned.

"Jess needs to be picked up again," I said.

There was silence and I felt her close the gap in her shirt with her hand. "I'm in a meeting, honey. Can you let the office know?"

"What if they need to talk to you? What if there's some kind of issue or something?"

"Then tell them to write a note and I'll sign it." My mom exhaled and I knew she was smoking a cigarette. Her voice drifted and broke up. "I'll be home late, so you girls just have dinner and get on to bed." I knew her meetings with Ben Bailey were not really meetings of the minds. They were meetings of something south, something that made my mom carry her panty hose home in her purse.

I pasted some graham crackers together with peanut butter and strawberry jelly and stacked them into paper towels. I felt numb in the head, like someone had shampooed me with Novocain. I wished I had more cheap dope so I could just eat a TV dinner and lie on the couch, leave Jess with her shows, sign for her homework, and go to bed. I could sleep until June, until registration for State College, until the last migration to the water, where we could smoke and drink and fuck and light fires. We were scattering after the summer and I was waiting. Dusty was going to Pittsburgh, Tim and Rich were heading south for football, and I was moving west, as close to the edge of the map as I could.

I drove to the junior high and parked in front of the main office. The parking lot was almost empty. The front door to the office was open and I walked in and stood at the counter. I recognized the secretary from when I used to go here. Her knit sweater was buttoned at her throat and she wore her glasses on a gold chain around her neck. Edna. Her name had been too hard to form a mean rhyme around when I was in seventh grade. We stuck our tongues out at her instead because we couldn't think of something to say.

She hit the computer keys in bursts and I finally cleared my throat so she'd look up. "Yes?" she said.

"I'm here for Jess Murphy," I said.

Edna eyed me up and down. She'd put on an even fifty since I'd seen her last and her glasses were buried like a pickax in the swell of her breasts. I had crammed for my last American history test and I knew sex with her would be like a Lewis and Clark expedition. She was wrapped in an orchid-print blouse and pastel yellow pants and her body was wide as the open prairie. She had a face like a hand-dug well. I let her raise her voice at me.

"We need a parent signature," she said. "The principal wants to have a conference." She wanted to punctuate her sentence with the computer keyboard, but I refused to step back from the counter. Her fingers were poised above home row but they did not move.

"I'm her guardian. I'm here to take her home."

I saw her index finger twitch but her wrists didn't bend. She ran her tongue across her top row of teeth and she dropped her hands to the desk. She took a deep breath and the orchid blouse swelled and rolled. "You'll have to talk to Ms. Peters. And you'll have to sign the form."

Jess came out from the principal's office and I slung her backpack over my shoulder. "I'll still need to speak to you," Ms. Peters said. She was the new principal and she liked to knot layers of sheer scarves over her throat. At Back to School Night I'd counted four, but then I realized it had been five—she had two that were the same shade of green.

Jess stood outside the office and I sat in the chair across from Ms. Peters's desk.

"Your sister needs a bathing suit," she said. "They're doing swimming in PE and it's mandatory that she participate." Ms. Peters ran a finger under a yellow scarf. "Unless she has a medical problem that prohibits her from the class. I've sent two letters to your house."

Our father was selling computer software in Detroit and sometimes he called on Sunday nights. My mom would start drinking early on Sundays and she'd wait for the phone to ring so she could keep telling him that she wasn't mad until she finally said she was goddamn mad and then she'd hang up on him. Sometimes he started drinking earlier than my mother, called her from Lansing, caught her off guard.

"My mom's been working a lot," I said. I thought about my mom and the restaurant leftovers in foil swans, Ben Bailey on the phone late at night. Ms. Peters's desk was light oak and nicked at the corners like someone had chipped at it with a knife.

"The school nurse is concerned about Jess," she said. "Her weight is a potential health problem."

I bit at my cuticles and spit the skin onto the stained carpet. I wondered if students had sat in front of Ms. Peters's desk and cried or puked or bled onto the carpet while she made phone calls and held conferences in that same controlled voice she used now and Edna typed in the other room. Jess was just over five-feet-four and she weighed 195 pounds the last time I'd seen her on a scale. She wore women's clothes and had to wear a bra because her fat tucked like breasts under her shirts.

"We want to help Jess. You understand, don't you?" she asked.

I carved a long flap of skin from the edge of my thumb and bit it off with my front teeth. Ms. Peters slid the forms across her desk. I spit the skin onto the papers and hoped the cut would bleed.

"I just need you to sign and acknowledge that you've been given the information regarding Jess's suspension if she doesn't participate in the spring PE activity. And that I notified you about her weight." I looked over my shoulder and saw Jess sitting in a chair outside the principal's office. She filled the chair and her thighs pushed out of the gaps beneath the armrests. *Notified.*

I signed the forms *Dolores Claiborne* and stood up from my chair. "Thank you," Ms. Peters said.

"Fuck you," I said, but I made sure I kept my voice low and my back turned.

"Excuse me?"

"No problem," I said.

We walked to the car and I threw Jess's backpack behind the seat. She got in and shut her door and I could hear her breathing in the quiet of the car. She was wearing gray sweats and tennis shoes, and she had her hair tucked behind her ears. She stared out the window and rubbed her hands back and forth on her thighs.

"Hungry?" I asked. I held the graham cracker sandwiches out to her but she didn't take them.

"I'm fine," she said. "Sorry about this."

I turned the radio off and drove in silence. Rain spattered the windshield and I could hear thunder rolling in the distance. I drove toward town. I parked in front of Penney's and waited for Jess to say something.

"I'll get you a suit," I said.

The rain was coming harder and I could barely see out the windshield with the wipers shut off. Jess pinched at the cotton pulled tight over her thighs but didn't look at me.

"We'll get something good," I said.

Jess took a deep breath and I could feel the seat shift beneath me. "Sam?" she said. "Could I maybe have one of those graham crackers?"

I handed her the paper towel and she took one of the sandwiches. We sat in the car and ate while the windows fogged up and we couldn't see the parking lot anymore.

We walked around the store and found the swimsuits. It was only April but an entire wall had been dedicated to summer wear. The mannequins were dressed in trunks and sunglasses, bikinis and cropped shirts. I skipped the bikini rack and went straight for the one-pieces. Jess followed behind me. I started with the larges, held one up, and then moved to the extra-larges. The selection wasn't good. Most of the extra-large suits had been designed like boat covers with a ruffle around the waist, and none of them looked like the kind of suit a twelve-year-old should wear to PE. I sifted through the rack and found one that might work. It was plain black and roomy, cut low on the legs with straps that were wide and didn't dip in the front or back.

"What d'you think?"

Jess shrugged her shoulders and I could see graham cracker crumbs in the corner of her mouth. I brushed off her lips and tucked a few strands of stray hair behind her ear. "It's no big deal, Jess," I said. "Try it on."

I took her to the fitting room and followed her into the small stall. She stood there without undressing and I leaned against the wall and waited. "C'mon," I said. I forgot that Jess didn't undress in front of anyone in the house. I hadn't seen her without a shirt for as long as I could remember.

"Can you wait outside?" she asked.

"I have to see how it looks. It might not be right. I'm your sister, for chrissake."

"Can't I take the suspension?" Her eyes were shiny under the bad lights.

"Jess, we can do this. It's just a bathing suit. It's just PE."

She shifted her weight back and forth on her feet and took the suit off the hanger. She held it up in front of her and looked in the mirror. "It seems small," she said.

"It stretches," I said.

She handed me the suit and turned her back to me. She pulled the sweatshirt over her head. When she raised her arms I could see her armpits with light hair reflected in the mirror. Dusty told me that fat kids go through puberty earlier. Dusty was my best friend and could tell me things like that. Jess started her period when she was ten. She dropped her sweatshirt to the floor. I could see the folds of skin that buried the straps of her bra. She stepped out of her shoes and pushed down her sweatpants. The skin on the backs of her legs was white and dimpled. There was a deep crease that ran from the front of her stomach and around her sides where her skin hung over the waistband of her underwear. She kept her eyes shut while she undressed.

"Take off your bra," I said.

She hesitated for a minute and then reached behind her and undid the clasp. Her breasts were full and streaked with purple stretch marks along the sides. I handed her the suit and she pulled it on. She wiggled her body into it, dipped her arms through the straps, and tried to tuck the elastic leg bands over her thighs. The bottom of her underwear puffed out. She turned around and held her arms up.

"Well?" she asked.

The spandex of the suit pulled tight across her belly so that it looked swollen under her soft breasts. The elastic bit into her thighs and shoulders—I knew it would leave marks in a matter of minutes. I tried to imagine her beside the heated pool with the whistle blowing and girls swimming laps and her trying to pull the leg holes of her suit loose from her thighs where the skin rubbed and the friction left a rash.

"It's okay," I said.

She pinched the material and let it snap back against her stomach. "It feels funny," she said.

"Maybe it's not a good fabric," I said. "Maybe we should try a better store."

Jess peeled free from the suit and I could hear the elastic snap at her skin. I waited for her to get dressed, then we left the swimsuit hanging in the room. It looked like a seal pelt on the wall.

I drove home without stopping at any more stores. Jess didn't say anything. The lights in Penney's had made me tired and I just wanted to make some soup and listen to the rain.

"Do you have a lot of homework tonight?" I asked.

"Math. The usual," she said.

"Mom's at a meeting. Maybe we could watch a movie on TV."

"Sure," she said.

In the weak wash of headlights Jess looked like she was six years old again, and I realized that she was only twelve, half her life was six years ago. I wanted to pull her across the seat and put my arm around her so she wasn't so exposed, so she could tuck her round face against my ribs and we could wait out the bad things. At twelve I had already sneaked a beer from the top shelf of the refrigerator, told my mom the bottle fell and broke when I was trying to put the milk carton away. And I learned that if one could fall, two could fall as well, and I gave Darren Webster a hand job in the movie theater during the last half of *Titanic*. He bought me popcorn and then he ignored me the next day. Jess had been little, growing out of her 6X pants, but still able to run, go to birthday parties, eat without people staring at her, wear a swimsuit, swim.

When we got home Jess sat at the kitchen table and watched me go through the cupboards to find something for dinner. The only kind of soup was cream of mushroom garlic. The wind threw handfuls of rain against the window and the lights flickered for a second and came back on again.

"Maybe we should light some candles," Jess said.

"Too bad we didn't have some scary movie to watch. And some soup."

Jess brought the candles out of the living room and dug matches out of the junk drawer. We turned the lights off and let the candles take over. I knew about the fat-camp brochures, the ones that Jess sent away for and hid in her room. I knew she was saving money so she could go. I watched her pocket the loose change from the couch cushions and add it to the jar in her room.

I opened the freezer and took out the carton of vanilla ice cream. I got a spoon out of the dishwasher—a soup spoon—and I set them both on the table in front of Jess. When Jess was younger our mom used to fix Jess's plate in the kitchen so she could control her portions. The food didn't fill the plate, just one scoop of everything, no seconds, no dessert. Jess used to cry in the night because she was hungry and her stomach hurt. I would crawl in bed with her and rub her belly in hopes that the weight of my hand would substitute for the food she couldn't have.

"Have some," I said.

Jess looked at the spoon and the ice cream and shook her head. "I'm not hungry," she said. "I'll wait for dinner."

The candles flickered on the countertops and the freezer

groaned and spit ice cubes into the tray. I pushed the carton closer to Jess. "Just eat it, Jess. It's okay."

Jess looked down at the table. "I said I'll wait for dinner."

"What if this is dinner? What if this could be dinner whenever you wanted?"

Jess pushed at the spoon and then folded her hands in front of her. "It can't. You know that."

"I think you're wrong. I don't think you know what you're missing."

"I'm missing PE, Sam. That's what I'm missing." Drops of water ran down the sides of the carton of ice cream.

"Take one bite," I said.

"Why're you doin' this, Sam? It's not funny."

"I'm not laughing. Just eat the ice cream, Jess. I promise that there's a point to all of this."

"That's what I'm waiting for. The point. I know the point."

I reached over and picked up one of her hands and rested it on the spoon. "It's a good thing, Jess. This is a good thing."

Jess looked at the ice cream container sweating in front of her and I smiled and pushed her hand down on the spoon. "Pretend it can be dinner," I said.

Jess picked up the spoon and dug it into the carton. She lifted out a full scoop of vanilla and put it in her mouth.

"It's good, right?" I said.

"Of course it's good. It's ice cream." She swallowed and set the spoon back on the table.

"Keep going," I said.

"I took a bite like you asked. I want to wait for dinner."

"This is dinner. Eat it."

Jess wiped the back of her hand across her mouth and stared

at me. I stood up from the table and took a piece of paper and a pen from next to the phone.

"What are you doing?" she asked. "Making a note for Mom that I ate all the ice cream? Recording the moment?"

"Take another bite," I said.

Jess picked the spoon up and scooped out another mouthful. She chewed the ice cream with her mouth open so I could see it.

"What do you want to have?" I asked.

"Spaghetti."

"Not for dinner, dummy. For PE. What's your medical excuse? The reason you can't take swimming."

Jess took another bite without my prompt. She smiled and there was a thin, sticky coat of milk on her lips. "Are you serious?"

"Absolutely. What do you have? What about a heart condition? No, that'll make that bitch principal think she's doing the right thing. A pulled ligament? Then you'll have to limp or something . . . I know—vertigo. You can't be in the water. It makes you dizzy."

"What's vertigo?"

"I don't know, it has to do with having your head spin and getting dizzy and feeling like you're gonna puke. This girl Vicky had it last year and she didn't even have to come to class."

Jess was scraping the sides of the carton. I could hear her spoon rubbing the cardboard clean. "Yeah, vertigo. I like it."

I wrote out the note to Ms. Peters and signed our mom's name. I could do her signature better than my own. Fat loop for L, swing the tail of the y around and hook it straight to the right side of the page. I gave the note to Jess and she shoved it into her back pocket. The spoon was tipped sideways in the carton and the ice cream was gone.

"Come with me," I said. I stood up and pulled Jess by the

sweatshirt so she'd follow me. I took her into the bathroom and turned on the light. "You have to trust me on this, okay? I mean really just trust me."

"What?" Jess leaned back against the sink and I pushed her toward the toilet and forced her to bend over. "What are you doing, Sam?" She tried to stand up but I kept my hand on her back and the other arm tight around her waist so I could lean against her.

"You get to eat the ice cream but you don't get to keep it."

"Let go of me," she said. She tried to force her weight into me, but I bent my knees and held my ground.

"Shhhhhhh. Just listen to me." I leaned in close to her ear so that my lips almost touched her skin. "You won't have to worry anymore," I whispered. "This will all go away." I gently squeezed the soft roll of her stomach with my hand. "And you can swim next year."

She was breathing hard and I could feel her chest rise and fall against me. I rubbed her back and kept my arm around her waist, my body pressed against her. Rich held Dusty like this once at a party when she drank shots for the first time, and Tim held me like this on his living-room carpet when his parents were at work, and I was holding Jess like this because it was April and in a few months I'd be gone. We both looked down at the toilet, the white seat, the clear water, the line of blue from the cube of bowl cleaner melting in the tank. "I'm scared," she said.

"I'll help you," I said. "We'll do this together."

No boy would ever roll his naked body into Jess in the dark on a school night, not like this, and she wouldn't know what it sounded like to hear him say he loved her, hear him say she was beautiful and good. I thought about our mom's panty hose in her purse and restaurant leftovers in foil swans and how a jar of change was just quarters and dimes that wouldn't buy fat camp or swimsuits that didn't rub rashes into thighs. I put two fingers up to her mouth and she opened wide for me, and I could feel the heat inside, the wetness and warmth, and I pushed my hand back until it had to curve downward to go further and I wiggled my fingers until she lurched against me and I bent over with her and held her as tight as I could.

She could learn to do this. It would be easy.

THE HISTORY
OF VEGAS

I had the taste of ashtray in my mouth, and every now and then my aunt Dolores farted in her sleep across the backseat of my mother's dirty Chevelle. "Your aunt Dolores is ill," my mom said when she saw me bite back a smile, and I looked out the window at miles of nothing and smiled anyway. The tires slapped freeway and I tried not to think about a cigarette. My mom smoked Viceroys down to the filters while she drove, but I couldn't light up while she was beside me. I sneaked a smoke in Bullhead City— told her I had to stretch my legs and then hit a Camel like it gave me oxygen instead of took it away. This trip was on account of my uncle Charlie and the fact that my aunt Dolores had a bruise around her eye that was bigger than a baseball. I heard my aunt Dolores crying in our apartment last night after I'd gone to bed, and this morning she was sitting in the kitchen drinking coffee with my mom. "We're going to Vegas," my mom told me while I poured Frosted Flakes into a bowl. "Get some clothes together."

I know she didn't want to take me on this trip, but my mom was in between boyfriends. She hated the last one too much to ask for a favor, and she didn't want to scare off the new one this early on by asking him to come by and check in on her son. As far as I knew, he didn't even know she had a seventeen-year-old in the house. I'd never seen the guy, but I had heard them come in late at night, heard ice dumped in glasses, and laughter. My mom had two kinds of laughter—the one that came deep from her lungs and bent her over with its force. It was the joke laughter. The laughter for funny things on TV. And there was the laughter late at night. The one that said, *No, stoppit*, but meant *Yes, keep right on going.*

She wouldn't leave me at home because my best friend, Mike, had a flavor for the five-finger discount. He couldn't help himself and my mom hated him coming around. She couldn't prove it, but she believed he took forty-six dollars of grocery money from the Folgers can in the cupboard. I didn't know if he did or not. Mike didn't drink coffee. She knew she could tell me to stay home and don't let anybody in and don't go out, but it was July. Everybody was out. And she didn't want me sucking down cigarettes in my bedroom at night, especially after Mrs. Brisbin's husband burned himself up in bed after he dropped a cigarette on the mattress. They had to evacuate the entire third floor of the building. I didn't know whether I should deny the fact that I was smoking or deny the fact that I would fall asleep with one in my hand. I denied the smoking and here I was, stuck in the Chevelle on U.S. 95 with half-hearted air-conditioning, static country on the radio, and Aunt Dolores making her own music in the backseat.

"Shit," my mom said, and she tipped her Viceroy into the ashtray. "The oil light's on again, Tommy. How much did you put in when we stopped for gas?"

"It was a good quart low," I said. The Chevelle dropped more oil than the state of Texas.

"Do you think we can make it with the light on? I don't want to have to pull off and take our chances on the side of the road." Flat, hard desert flanked both sides of the car. The highway shimmered like a broken bottle edge on the beach. It was empty in both directions.

"The light measures *pressure*, not *quarts*. I don't know how much is in the pan. We have to conserve on the pressure. Maybe we'll make it to the next gas station. I don't know." I licked my lips and my tongue came away dry.

"Okay, then. Shut everything down that we don't need."

I switched off the radio and sat back in my seat. My mom pulled the lever on the air-conditioning.

"You said what we *don't* need. We need the air-conditioning, Mom. We're in the desert, for chrissake."

"We have windows. Roll them down."

We both cranked the knobs on our windows and dry desert air filled the car with heat. It felt like someone had hooked a fan up to the sun. I was sweating across my upper lip and the wind just spread the beads out until my whole face was shiny in the side mirror.

Aunt Dolores sat up in the back. Her eye was swollen shut and she had the seam of the vinyl seat across her cheek. "What's going on?" she asked.

"The damn car is running through the oil again and we aren't gonna make it to Vegas if we don't cut the air conditioner. I'm sorry, hon, but it's either this or we sit on the side of the highway with nothing moving at all," my mom said.

"How much further?"

"A sign said sixty-two miles a while back. I don't know, fifty miles? Less?"

Aunt Dolores tried to smooth her hair out of her face, but the wind caught the strands and pushed them back again.

"Just sit back and don't worry about anything. We're gonna be in Vegas before the lights come up, and then me and you are gonna hit the town," my mom said.

Aunt Dolores smiled and closed her good eye. The other eye was the color of twilight before the streetlights kick on.

The sun was sliding past noon when my mom eased the car onto Las Vegas Boulevard and made the left on Sahara. She had booked us into the Silver Slipper, just off the Strip, because Elvis was doing three shows over the weekend and my aunt Dolores was a huge fan of the King. There were four dollars left in the coffee can back home and Elvis might get our grocery money for the month. I just hoped Vegas wasn't getting our rent money, too.

The Silver Slipper wasn't a tall building like the other hotels and casinos. Instead, the casino faced the main street and behind it was a set of low buildings that went back for a full city block. The low buildings in back were the rooms, motel style, with two floors and three swimming pools and parking in front. I waited in the car while my mom and Aunt Dolores checked in at the lobby and then my mother handed me a map of the rooms with number 562 circled in bright orange ink. We were at the far end of the buildings, upstairs, two double beds, smoking room.

I carried the suitcases and my mom unlocked the door. The beds were against the right wall and the window faced the parking lot. The carpet was green shag and the bedspreads were brown and red striped. There was a television on the heavy three-drawer dresser on the opposite wall from the beds, and a small round table under the window with two swivel chairs against it. There were four ashtrays and a King James Bible beside the phone.

"You take the bed closest to the window," my mom said.

I dropped my bag on the bed and turned on the television.

"Get comfortable with that television, Tommy. That's gonna be your company for the next few days."

"Now let's freshen up and get out of this room," my mom said.

Aunt Dolores blew her nose and thumbed mascara from under her eye. "Okay," she said.

I finally gave in and watched game shows while they showered and blow-dried, sprayed, powdered, painted, ironed, and perfumed. I had seen the routine a million times, but I still didn't know how women could take so long just to get out the door. In the time it took my mother to put her eye makeup on, I watched a man from Florida win two thousand dollars with Nipsey Russell on *Rhyme and Reason*. My aunt Dolores put on a sundress with blue dots. She had a pair of brown glasses with big round lenses like Farrah Fawcett wore on *Charlie's Angels*. If that show was on, I could definitely kill some time alone in the room.

"Do I look okay, Carol?" Aunt Dolores asked. She put on the glasses and stood up so my mom could see her.

"You look absolutely beautiful," my mother said.

"What about the glasses? Too obvious?" she asked.

"They're like Hollywood, hon. Star quality. Right, Tommy?"

Aunt Dolores turned toward me and I could see my mother pinch her lips together over Aunt Dolores's shoulder and jerk her head in a way that was supposed to signal that I should say something good.

"You look like Farrah Fawcett," I said. My mom relaxed her face and smiled her approval. In a way, Aunt Dolores kind of did look like Farrah Fawcett, if I squinted my eyes and looked at her through my lashes. She had blond hair that was brushed back from the sides of her face. But her shoulders were rounded forward like she wasn't used to standing up straight.

"I don't look *that* good," she said. The trace of a smile crossed her face, and in that moment I wanted to believe she looked that good for her sake.

The rabbit ears on the television were bent and I could get decent reception on only three stations. *I Love Lucy, The Dating Game,* or news. I flicked the TV off and kicked back onto my bed with my feet up. My mom pulled the heavy flowered drapes closed and lit a cigarette. She turned the air conditioner to high and spread her arms wide in front of the vent.

"So what do I do now?" I asked.

"God, Tommy. We just got here, and for your information, this trip isn't for your entertainment. It's for your aunt Dolores. Watch TV. Take a nap. I don't care."

Aunt Dolores sat on the end of their bed with her head resting in her hands. My mom sat down and rubbed Aunt Dolores's back. "I'll make that phone call in the morning. I already talked to his secretary and he can get us in before the weekend is up. It's just paperwork to file, a couple of fees to pay, and that's it, hon. That's all she wrote."

I could tell my aunt was crying by the way her ribs moved. She kept her head down and sniffed quietly. "Shhhhh. This isn't a time to cry, Dee. This is a time to paint the town and have some fun. Like we talked about. Everything is just like we talked about."

Aunt Dolores didn't look up. "I just run my mouth too much, Carol. I know it. Charlie tells me to shut it up, but I push it too far. It's my own fault. I just don't quit."

"It ain't your fault at all, Dee. Charlie doesn't have the right to send you out in the night, with an eye puffed shut and no money in your purse. This is the last time. Three strikes and you're out. Just like that. You know I'm right, don't you, hon? This is the best thing to do. You know this is all exactly how it's supposed to be," my mom said.

Aunt Dolores nodded her head slowly and my mom stood up to pull some tissue from the box by the bathroom sink.

"We'll have to fight the men off," my mom said. She held her hand up to shield Aunt Dolores's face and sprayed her head with a heavy dose of Aquanet. I coughed and put my pillow over my face.

"Okay, Tommy, we'll get out of your hair and leave you with your television," my mom said. She opened her purse and took out a ten-dollar bill. "This is for dinner and some snack stuff for the room. Make it last because this is your money for the next few days. There's a burger place next door and I'll leave you a room key. Go there and back. I don't want you out walking around, and if they catch you in a casino, they'll call the police on you, so don't try it. Let me trust you, huh, Tommy? Do it for your aunt Dolores."

I took the money and shoved it into the front pocket of my jeans. I wanted to argue for more money, but ten dollars would get me some cigarettes and some food, so I thought it best to take what was offered and keep my mouth shut. If I got into it with her, they might stick around the room for God knew how long, and then I'd never get out for some smokes.

"Don't worry so much about me," I said. "Go have fun."

My mom bent over and kissed me on the cheek and I wiped it off with the back of my hand. It came away with a smear of lipstick. My mom slid a room key into her purse and opened the door. "Don't wait up for us, Tommy," she said. "There aren't any clocks in Vegas."

I watched them through the slit in the drapes and waited until they disappeared around the corner of the building. I laced up my tennis shoes and left the room. The heat blasted me like I had pulled the door open on a furnace. I bent my arm across my eyes until I could adjust to the sudden brightness of light reflecting off the white buildings, car metal, asphalt. I didn't have sunglasses and there was no way I was going to dip into my ten bucks for some.

I wasn't hungry, so I walked east toward the Strip and the stark buildings that were naked in the daylight. Vegas was dirty in the sunshine. It had all of the charm of Christmas lights hanging off of rafters in midafternoon. But even in the heat the sidewalks were crowded. People moved slowly, like they weren't in any hurry to get under the air-conditioning of a dim casino and start pumping the machines with their car payment. Within a block, my T-shirt was stuck to my back. In two blocks I could feel sweat soaking through the armpits.

I found a souvenir store and bought a pack of Camels. I lit one out front and thought about walking back to the motel until the sun went down, but then this girl walked up and asked for one of my smokes and I decided to stay out for a while.

"You from around here?" she asked.

"No," I said. "You?"

"I'm from around." She was wearing mirrored sunglasses, so I couldn't see her eyes, but I knew she was looking right at me. I shifted my feet and pretended to be absorbed in watching the cars go by.

I couldn't tell how old she was, but she looked young—there was something about the shape of her face that made her look like she hadn't lost all her baby fat yet. I dropped my eyes from her face for a second and took a quick look at the front of her shirt. She had on a tight red tee and a pair of denim cutoffs that were cut so short, the white corners of the front pockets stuck out below the jagged hem. Her small feet were strapped into a pair of platforms that boosted her a good four inches above her real height.

"I like your necklace," I said.

"I bet you do."

I stared down at my shoes, like they were the most interesting pair of black canvas sneakers that I had ever seen. "How old are you?" I asked.

"How old are *you*?" She exhaled and flicked ash onto the sidewalk.

"Seventeen," I said.

"Really? Me, too."

I smoked my cigarette down to nothing and dropped it on the sidewalk so I could toe it out. I waited for her to say something, but she just stood there smoking like the silence didn't bother her at all.

"Well," I said. "I guess I'll go back to my room."

"Where're you stayin'?"

"Over at the Silver Slipper. Upstairs. In the back." I didn't know why I added the information, but it was like I couldn't stop talking once it was my turn.

"You by yourself?" she asked.

"No. I mean yes. Sort of. No one's at the room. No one will be back until late."

"It sure is hot out here," she said.

"We've got AC in the room. I cranked it up as high as it will go."

She looked up at me with those shiny glasses and I could see a smaller version of myself reflected back.

"So you want me to go back to the room with you?" she asked.

My head felt light from the heat and the cigarette. I rubbed my eyes and tried to get my focus back.

"Yeah. Sure. I mean, if you want and all. We could watch some TV. Sit under the AC."

"That would be nice," she said. "What's your name?"

"Tommy."

"Okay, Tommy. Why don't you go back in the store and get us

another pack of cigarettes and something to drink. I'll wait right here for you."

The room was cool and dark inside and I sat down on my bed and offered her a Coke from the six-pack I'd bought. She sat across from me on the other bed and leaned her weight back against her outstretched arms.

"You want to watch some television?" I asked.

"Whatever," she said.

I turned the dial and adjusted the rabbit ears. The game shows came in the best and I sat back on the bed to watch a woman spin the reels on *The Joker's Wild*. The air conditioner rattled in the wall.

"You mind if I take off my shoes?" she asked.

"No. Go ahead. Make yourself at home."

She unbuckled her sandals and looked around the room. "You here with your mom?"

"And my aunt Dolores," I said. I almost told her about the eye, but then stopped and took a sip from my Coke.

"I bet your mom wouldn't like it if she knew you had a girl up here, huh?"

I didn't say anything. The reels stopped and Jack asked the fifty-dollar question.

She stood up and came over to me. She pushed me back onto the bedspread and pulled my shoes and socks off. I sat my Coke on the little table between the beds.

"Isn't that better?" she asked.

She pulled me into a semi-sitting position and grabbed the bottom of my T-shirt. She tugged it up and over my head.

"How 'bout that?" she asked.

I reached out and touched both of her arms. They were cool and thin. I could feel the bones underneath.

She leaned forward and kissed my neck. Her breath was hot and I could feel her eyelashes brush against my skin. She unbuttoned my jeans and stretched the opening wide so the zipper was forced down. I was straining at the elastic band of my underwear. She scooted sideways off the bed and slid her shorts down. Her panties were bright blue with a thin string that went over her hipbones and connected the front to the back. She hitched her fingers under the string and stepped out of them. I looked up at the ceiling, but not before I saw the patch of light hair between her legs.

"Have you ever done this before?" she whispered.

I thought about the time I made out with Lorraine in her living room when her dad was at work, how I had been on top of her and she let me keep going—I was so amazed that her hands never once pushed me away—and then she told me to use a rubber and I had one, just one, in my wallet, and as I tried to roll it on I got nervous, or maybe it was just the fact that she let me touch it against her for just a second, skin on skin, and as I rolled the rubber on I came so quickly I didn't even have time to turn away from her or breathe. It was just over and I was sorry and she said, "It's okay, it's no big deal."

"Yes," I said now.

She straddled her leg on the other side of me and eased my underwear down enough to grip me and guide me inside.

We smoked cigarettes and watched game shows. She told me her name was Trish and her parents were getting a divorce and everything was shit at home. She didn't have much money or any place to stay that didn't last for more than a day or two. Her friends couldn't keep taking her in.

"Maybe my mom could help you out," I said. "She won't just kick you out of here if she knows you're in trouble."

"I don't know, Tommy. I don't think it's a good idea. But it's sweet that you'd think about it."

"We could take you back with us. You could get a job or something."

She laughed and pulled the sheet higher against her chest. "You're somethin' else, you know that?" I kissed her and ran a hand down her bare thigh against me.

The knock on the door was so loud that I dropped my cigarette onto the bed and had to pick it up and flick the ash off before it cinged. I thought of Mr. Brisbin waking up on fire.

I set the cigarette in the ashtray and pulled on my jeans. The knock came again, loud and hard. I looked through the peephole out to the landing and saw a guy with slick dark hair and a suit.

"Shit," I said.

"Is it your mother?" Trish asked. She leaned over the bed and started gathering up her clothes.

"No, no. Just stay still."

I unhooked the chain and cracked the door open. I squinted my eyes against the light.

"Hey, hey, Tommy. Surprise, huh?"

"What're you doing here, Uncle Charlie?" I took a step out onto the landing, but the cement was hot against my bare feet. Charlie tried to catch a look inside the room and I pulled the door closer to me.

"It's fuckin' hot out here, Tommy. Open up and let me in."

"I can't right now, Uncle Charlie," I said.

"Can't? What is that, can't? I been in the car for hours and you can't let me in the room? That's not what family says, Tommy." Charlie shoved his hands in his front pockets and turned so he could spit over the railing. "Dolores in there?" he asked.

"Nah. Her and Mom went out. They said they'd be back late."

"Out, huh? Okay." Charlie was wearing a powder blue suit, jacket and all, but he wasn't so much as breaking a sweat. "Come and get a soda or something with me. What d'ya say?"

I looked over my shoulder at Trish in the bed. Uncle Charlie settled his weight back on his heels and breathed through his nose.

"Who's in the room, Tommy? You said your mom and Dolores are out."

"They are," I said.

Charlie looked at me for a minute and then he smiled. His smile was so wide that I could see the fillings in his back teeth.

"Oh, I get it, Tommy. Jesus, excuse me for interrupting you. I forget that you ain't so much a kid no more." He held his hands out and shrugged. "One drink with your uncle, though. Huh? Please?"

I shifted my weight onto one foot and scratched my bare chest. Maybe he'd have a drink and go. Maybe I could say something to let him know that Aunt Dolores would be home in a few days. She just needed some time.

"Okay. But Trish comes with us," I said.

Charlie pursed his lips together. "Sure. Trish comes, too. You two get yourselves composed and I'll wait for you."

We got dressed and met Charlie on the landing. He was leaning against the railing and watching the parking lot.

"Ready," he said.

"There's a burger place next door," I said. "We could have a Coke over there."

"We don't want a burger place, Tommy. We can do better than that. Let's take a ride. You've never been in my Crown Vic. Leather seats, air-conditioning. We'll get out of this sun."

We followed him to a maroon car parked near the building. There was a man in the front seat and I recognized him as Joe Santini, the guy who helped run the pawn shop with Uncle Charlie—Cabassi Jewelry and Loan. Trish and I got into the backseat and Uncle Charlie slid behind the wheel.

"You remember Joe," he said. Joe turned around and nodded his head toward each of us.

"So the women went out, huh, Tommy?" Uncle Charlie eased the Crown Vic out of the space and guided it toward the exit. The car was cold inside and smelled like new dress shoes.

"I don't know where," I said. Trish squeezed my hand and I rubbed my thumb against hers.

Charlie stopped talking and drove west away from the Strip, and the casinos thinned out and gave way to liquor stores, discount shops, auto garages. I watched streets go by in silence.

Charlie pulled the car to the curb in front of an empty restaurant with boards on the windows. He let the motor idle and he turned in his seat so he could face us.

"How much is your game?" he asked Trish.

Trish stared out the window and didn't say anything.

"C'mon, honey. How much you running him?" Charlie asked.

I just sat there with my hand sweating into hers. I felt her grip loosen on my fingers and her hand slipped away.

"Fifty," she said. I looked at her and shook my head. I didn't know what she meant.

Charlie pulled a money clip from the inside of his suit jacket and peeled two twenties and a ten off the stack. He thought for a second, put the ten back, and peeled off another twenty. He handed the money across the seat to Trish. "Beat it. End of the line." He turned forward in his seat and looked out the windshield.

Trish lifted the door handle and swung her legs out to the curb.

"Hey," I said. "What the hell is going on?"

"Sorry," she said. She stepped out and pushed the door closed. Charlie hit the gas pedal and the Crown Vic swerved away from the curb. I jerked my head around in time to see Trish shove the money down the front of her shirt and walk back in the direction of the Strip.

"Can someone tell me what just happened?" I asked.

"Gotta pay to play, Tommy. Shit, Joe, that jailbait would've taken him for three times that if we hadn't stepped in," Charlie said. Joe snorted in agreement.

"You know, Tommy, it ain't your fault, what with how your mother raised you and all, but you don't know shit about women. Now, I don't mean to disrespect your mom—hell, I'd shoot a guy for looking cross-eyed at my own—but you've got to know a few things." We cut through neighborhoods and settled onto two-lane blacktop that continued west through the outskirts of town.

"See, your mom has all these wrong ideas about Dolores. She doesn't know that Dolores doesn't want for nothing. She has everything she asks for. The only problem is that she don't know when to stop running her mouth and nagging at me. See, where I grew up, that kind of woman was called a bitch and she had to be knocked down a peg or two to remind her just who paid the bills in the house. Not everything I do is her fucking business."

The road was empty and the buildings were behind us. The windows looked out on scrub weeds and sand. "I thought we were going to get a drink, Uncle Charlie. Me and you."

"Yeah, we'll do that, Tommy, but I wanna take you for a ride in my new car. What d'ya think of this Crown Vic, huh?"

"It's great," I said.

"'Great'? Shit, it's about the best goddamn car you can buy."

Charlie tapped the speedometer up to seventy and I thought I could feel the engine through the floorboards.

"Your mother's been like this since you was a kid and your father was around." At the mention of my father I held my breath and sat up straighter in the seat. "She drove your father away. You know that, don't you?" When I was seven years old my mom told me that my father was the kind of guy who couldn't stick. In my head I saw him as a piece of gum covered in pocket lint.

"I met Dolores in Vegas. How 'bout that? She was cocktailing and I was doing some work for Lou Massino—overseeing the pit at the Flamingo, shit like that. You believe that, Joe? Me, back in the day, dropped right in the middle of the Flamingo with those old-timers. They told me to jump, I said how the fuck high for about a week, and then I earned my place and they didn't say boo," Charlie said. Joe laughed and rolled a toothpick to the corner of his mouth.

"So fucking what," I said. I clenched my jaw after the words came out and wished I could suck them right back in, but I was getting tired of listening to Charlie put down my mom, and for no reason in particular, my balls were trying to crawl up into the pit of my stomach. I didn't like the way I felt.

"You hear the mouth on him?" Charlie nodded my direction. Joe shook his head like he was ashamed for me. "How old are you, Tommy?" Charlie asked.

"Seventeen."

"Jesus, seventeen. If I was your father I'd cauliflower your ear.

I was fifteen when my old man put my own blood on my shirt. It only took one time. After that I moved out and got a job working for Lou. Lou was like a father to me. My old man didn't even take me fishing when I was kid. It was Lou who did all that shit for me. He gave me some jobs to do, I did them right, and then he sent me out to Vegas and the next thing I know, other men—men older than me—are calling me sir and walking around with their dicks in their hands if I told them to. Jesus, that was years ago." Charlie settled his arm against the back of the seat. I could see his gold watch wink out from his shirt cuff. "What I'm saying, Tommy, is that there's history here, my history, and your mom doesn't know shit about it."

My hands were sweating against the seat leather and I tried to rub them dry on my jeans. The sun was dipped low in the sky and the clouds in the distance were bruised like ripe fruit underneath.

"I should be getting back, Uncle Charlie," I said. "We could all get some dinner. Me and you and Mom and Aunt Dolores. And Joe, too."

Charlie didn't say anything. Joe cleared his throat and drummed his fingers against his knees.

"Did your mom make any phone calls in the room?" Charlie asked.

I thought for a second and shook my head. I could see Charlie looking at me in the rearview mirror and I dropped my eyes to my lap. "No. There weren't any phone calls."

"Dolores is everything to me, you know that, Tommy? We made a commitment to each other—sacred vows in front of God and Lou and everybody in a chapel right here in Vegas—and we promised that nothing would come between us. 'Till death do we part.' That means we don't just walk, Tommy. And Dolores knows that. But your mom, she don't quite have that all figured out yet. She can't just come in and take what belongs to me—take what I love."

I felt the car slow and Charlie turned off the two-lane road and onto another road that wasn't paved. The tires kicked up small rocks that pinged against the fenders. I had the taste of ashtray in my mouth again, but I didn't want a cigarette. I wanted to be back in the motel room with the television on, watching someone spin the reels for Jack.

"There's a lesson in everything, Tommy," Charlie said. He had both hands on the wheel and the car was fishtailing in the soft sand. "What was it that fuck stick said, Joe? That guy on that show? You don't need eyes, you need a vision. That's a lesson, Tommy. It means everything is in your fucking head. Everything you see."

The car climbed a small incline and then dropped down. The dunes around us were naked and bleached white as underbelly. Charlie tapped the brake and the wheel pulled to the left as the car came to a stop. He put the car in park and turned the ignition off. I couldn't see the main road behind us. There was nothing but desert and the slow tick of the engine as it cooled.

"Why are we stopping here?" I asked. My voice cracked and I cleared my throat. "Uncle Charlie?"

Charlie and Joe stepped out of the car. Charlie pulled my door open and motioned for me to join them. The air was hot, but there was a slight wind that moved across the flat expanse around us. I could smell the dampness of earth and something deeper like rain. Charlie put his arm around my shoulder and guided me toward the front of the car. He turned me so that I looked out at the horizon and could see the burnt oranges, pinks, and greens of the sunset. "The desert is a beautiful place," Charlie said. "It's like one big secret." The wind lifted my hair off the back of my neck and the sweat dried to my skin. I remembered when I was five years old and I stole a Baby Ruth from Woolworth's while my mom was shopping, and for the next two days every time there were sirens going by she would tell me, "They're coming for you, Tommy. Here they come."

SUPPLEMENT

When harvest time came in early summer, the Mexicans drove their rusted-out cars into our driveway and lined up for work. My dad would hire fifteen or twenty, sometimes more, and they'd work for cash paid out every day until the last head of scrub lettuce or sugar beet was pulled from the ground. I had to help my mother pack lunches and drive them out to the fields where the Mexicans worked. I'd sit on the tailgate while she drove down the row and then I'd pass the brown bags out. We made sure they had water jugs they could fill at the sprinkler pump. Once when we drove down to the fields there were a bunch of them standing in a group, and when my mother stopped the pickup they just stood there, looking down at the ground. I thought maybe someone had fainted—they did that sometimes, took the sun in their face too long, wouldn't stop for water—but then one ran up and started yelling *"bebé"* and my mother threw her door open.

There was a woman on the ground and her legs were bent. She had short hair and didn't look much like a woman—no one had even thought she was pregnant—but she was on the ground with her head tipped back and her baggy work pants were dark with wetness below the waist. "Get behind her, Jaycee. Lift her head off the dirt," my mother yelled at me, and I pushed past the men and got down on my knees so I could lift her head to my lap. Her face was mud-streaked and sweaty, and she was talking low in fast Spanish I couldn't understand. My mother unbuttoned the woman's pants and the men stepped back some, and I could see everything below her waist, her dark skin and bare legs, the hair, the blood on the inside of her thighs. "I'm gonna try and find a blanket or something in the truck," my mother said and ran. The woman was breathing hard and I could smell her breath, like grass after a rain, and I leaned closer to her face in the hopes I could understand something and help her, tell her she was okay. The tendons stood out on her neck and I smoothed her hair back from her forehead, and I watched the insides of her thighs, the way the muscles tensed and shook like a horse's flank lifting a fly, and I knew that her skin was soft over her thighs, that if I touched it, it would be soft and warm under my hand.

She birthed the baby onto two jackets and a work shirt. My mother pulled the baby out in three hard contractions and then the men clapped. "Unbutton her shirt," my mother told me, and I did, slipped the plastic button through the holes so that the shirt fell open on both sides of her. She didn't have a bra underneath and her breasts were that same soft brown color as her tights, the nipples dark and large, and my mother raised the baby from the jackets, wrapped him on the inside of the shirt he was born on, and put him against the woman's chest. The baby was still wet and stained. "Help him," my mother said, and I guided his head toward the woman's breasts, watched his lips move to suck even before his mouth closed on a nipple. I watched him nurse, his cheeks pulling tight, while my mother sent one of the men back to the house to call for more help.

My mother named me Jaycee after her sister. My mother said that Aunt Jaycee was a wanderer. She could never settle down. I knew my mother had that restlessness. There was something inside her that made it hard to be around her. When it wasn't harvest time she would stay in the house all day, and after that Mexican had the baby in the field, my father stopped hiring women and there was a fight between him and my mother that hasn't ever come to an end. At dinner she would sit and stare out across the table. The chicken would be half-cooked and my father would yell so that I would have to put the plates in the microwave until the pink was gone. Sometimes she only pushed the food around her plate to make it look like she'd eaten some of it. When she went to town I would think, This is the time. This is when she won't come back. I would watch the clock. After two or three hours I would pace around and feel the armpits of my shirt turn damp and cold. Then I'd hear the truck come up the driveway and my mother would slam the door and yell for some help with the groceries. I knew she pretended. She didn't know that I knew. She complained that her bed was too hard for her back, so she slept in my brother Brett's room and Brett moved into a sleeping bag on the floor in mine.

My father was down in the pens docking the sheep with the neighbor men from up the road, and he wanted beer now, sent me to bring it because I was a girl and girls run and bring things. Girls don't stand in the pens where the lambs wear shit like waders and everything smells like blood on a wet wool blanket.

I didn't feel like walking all the way up to our house for beer, so I walked over to Husso's instead. He and his wife rented a little shack on our property. I don't think they paid any money to my father since Husso was hired to work the sheep, but maybe part of the work was trade. The shack wasn't bad—it was west of our house and off by itself under a scatter of oak trees. It had two rooms and a bathroom, and a little kitchen with a sink, stove, and refrigerator.

I was jealous when my father let Husso and Betsy move in there. I had wanted it to be my apartment away from the house.

I knocked on the door and Betsy answered. She had been married to Husso for four years. She was Mexican with long straight black hair, but her face was the color of clean bone, not the dirt color of the field workers. Her eyes were dark and large and always soft around the edges, like everything needed sympathy. Her nose was a straight line in her narrow face. She was twenty-five and Husso was almost forty.

"Do you have any beer, Betsy? My dad asked me to make a run up to the house, but I thought I'd try here first."

Betsy pushed the door open and let me in. She had a fire going in the woodstove and I realized how cold the air was this far from the docking coals in the pen. I could hear a pot bubbling and smell chili, the air burned sharp with spice and tomato.

"Of course we have beer. You think Husso would let me run the house without making sure we had the necessities?" She smiled and I could see the chip in her front tooth. She had told me that on her first date with Husso he took her hunting out on a back road. His friend drove the truck slow and they would jump off the tailgate to shoot at doves. One time she went to jump back on and misjudged the distance. She slipped and hit her face on the bed of the truck as she jumped in. She broke her nose, split her lip, and chipped her tooth. If Husso hadn't grabbed her, she would've rolled out onto the road and probably split her head open as well. She said she fell in love with him after that.

"My dad wants one, but that'll mean two by the time I get back out to the pen. They're almost done down there. I asked Husso if he wanted one, but he didn't answer."

"Take him two. When he says nothing it means yes."

"Why aren't you down there watching?" I asked.

Betsy opened the refrigerator and took out a six-pack of bottles. "I would like to be able to kiss Husso again someday." Husso was Basque and liked to show off to the neighbors by biting through the lamb's balls with his teeth instead of pulling tight and cutting the skin with a knife. Down by farm there were neighbors leaning up against the fence around the pens, and the testicles were coiled in tubes on the dirt. Husso's chin was slick with blood.

"I can't see how you can," I said.

"I can't seem to stop."

I took the pack of Pabst and opened the door. Betsy reached out and touched my hair. I could feel her fingers lift and slide through the strands until they reached the ends and my hair fell back against my neck. A shiver made its way up my spine. "Come back later and let me do your hair," she said. "I want to try a new braid I learned." Betsy read a lot of hairstyle magazines. She wanted to get her cosmetology license, but she wasn't sure that Husso would let her take their only truck into town every day. He liked her home.

The wives were tired of watching the work and they had retreated to the open doors of the pickups so they could run the heaters and talk about canning and kids and husbands and grocery prices. My mother was up at the house with the television on. I held the six-pack over the top board of the fence and yelled to my father.

"Just pull me out one and bring it in here," he said.

I climbed into the pen with a bottle. The lambs on the other side of the chute shook and opened their mouths without a sound. Small puffs of steam came out of their mud-caked nostrils. The shit-mud sucked at my boots.

My father took the beer and drank it without stopping for a

breath. "Three lambs to go," he said. "Keep them beers close to the fence."

Husso climbed out of the pen and hawked a mouthful of spit onto the ground, then toed dirt over it with his boot. He lifted his T-shirt and wiped at his face, but there were so many layers of blood that only some of it separated into a dark smear on his shirt. He took a beer and wiped the bottle against his cheeks and chin. The sticky darkness around his mouth spread thin.

"S'damn shame we only do this a few times a year, huh?" he said. Some of the wives kicked clods of mud toward him and he winked at me. He held the bottle in his left hand, with only his thumb and two fingers around the neck. The other fingers had been fed to a hay bailer when Husso was twenty. Brett said that Husso lost his fingers in a knife game, but Brett didn't know everything. Both fingers were taken off at the knuckle. Sometimes I wondered what Betsy felt when he touched her—if she could feel the absence of his fingers when he touched her skin, ran his hand across her thigh in bed. I wondered if he could bend the stubs, if they just felt small against her.

Husso put his hand—the one with five fingers—against the small of my back and I could feel the heat through my shirt. I could smell the blood on him, that copper smell like a wet penny and sweat.

"Next time maybe you should hold the babies for the castrating," he said. "It'll keep you from looking at the boys for a while." I felt his hand press into my back and his pinkie finger spread wide enough to slip under the waist of my jeans.

"I have to get this beer in the shade," I said. I stepped away from him and his fingers pulled free.

"Hey, Frank," Husso yelled to my father. "Hurry up, you old

man. It's time to turn those son of a bitches back to the barn and have happy hour."

Brett's hair was in wet points under his baseball cap and he tried to knock some of the dirt from his jeans when he came out from the pen. He was built more like Husso than he was like either my father or my mother. He was tall and thin, but with broad shoulders and a square jaw. I didn't think Husso was that strong at first, but I had seen him carry two fifty-pound grain sacks over each shoulder and throw down hay bales faster than my father. I watched him string fences, pull the wire so tight it wouldn't move against the post.

"Here," Husso said. He handed Brett a beer.

Brett twisted the top and tried not to look to see if our father was watching, but I felt his eyes slide back toward the pen like he couldn't help himself. He drank the beer fast, but I don't think it was just because he was thirsty.

"Six for milk," Husso said to Brett. "You better get your ass back to work or you're gonna be penning lambs by flashlight." Some of the ewes had birthed twins and one of the lambs would go hungry if we didn't supplement their milk and bottle-feed. Husso pulled another beer bottle out and put the cap in his front pocket after he opened it.

"I've been here all day," Brett said. "Jaycee hasn't done anything. She can do it."

"She brought the beer," Husso said. "That's what the women do."

"Actually, Husso, I took the beer from your house," I said.

"Son of a bitch. Give it back, then, huh?" Husso took the beer out of Brett's hand.

"I'll help. Jesus. I always have to split shit with her," Brett said.

"Okay," Husso said. He gave the beer back to Brett. "You drink my beer, then you help the girl. You're the one who will get all this farm someday. It's not her place to do the work." I could feel his hand on my back again and the fingers moved in small circles so that my shirt wrinkled and pulled tight beneath them.

Betsy walked up and I felt Husso's hand slide off my back like a fish sinking from the surface of a pond. There were clouds stacking up against the mountains and the sky had dulled. Betsy's hair soaked up the sunlight.

"I brought this up for you, baby," Betsy said. She handed Husso a wet washcloth. Husso scrubbed at his face and handed it back to her. There were still dark flecks around the corners of his lips. "Hold still," she said. She held the washcloth against the tip of her finger and rubbed it against his lips until he was clean. I wondered what it felt like to have someone take such close care, then she leaned forward and kissed him. She pushed her body against his and I saw her mouth relax and open so she could take his tongue, and then I looked away.

The dark edges of the lamb's mouth bubbled wet and white while I tipped the goats' milk bottle. The goats didn't miss the milk and the lambs didn't notice the difference. While the lambs nursed the rubber nipple, the sky had gone gray and there were no crickets out to fiddle sound into the smell of rain.

Husso was up at the barn fixing a tractor when I walked over to their house. The barn was bright with the overhead lights and I could hear the low talk of men and the occasional sound of a tool being turned against metal. Betsy answered the door and I went inside.

"You want to listen to music?" she asked.

Betsy lit some candles and turned on the small portable stereo plugged into the wall. A woman's voice came on. It was rough and low and sounded like it came from deep in her lungs. I wondered how she could keep from coughing with that many wet-sounding edges in her throat. There was oak wood burning in the stove and I could hear pitch pop and sputter beneath the rub of the woman's voice.

"I want to wash your hair first," Betsy said.

She had me sit in a tall chair with my back against the sink. She bent my head toward the faucet and I closed my eyes. I felt the warm water seep down into my scalp.

"Is it too hot?" Betsy asked.

"No. It's good," I said. "It's perfect."

Betsy ran her fingers through my hair and lifted it under the running water. She cupped the water in her hands and let it soak into the thicker hair against my neck. Her hands kept moving the water away from my face and I closed my eyes.

"This is good shampoo," she said.

I just made a humming noise with my lips. I could smell lavender and vanilla. Betsy scrubbed my scalp with the tips of her fingers, all ten of them bent firm against my head. I could feel her lift sections of my hair so she could scrub them in layers, holding some in one palm and scrubbing at them with her other hand. She moved her fingers slow against my neck. She talked to me, but her words ran together like the water from the taps.

When she finished, she lifted my head from the lip of the sink and toweled it dry. My head felt like it was too heavy for my neck to hold up. I felt tired, like I could just lie down on the couch and sleep until the sun came up. Part of me wanted to lay my head in Betsy's lap and have her fingers keep touching my head.

"You want something to drink?" she asked.

I nodded and sat down on the couch. Betsy brought me a full

water glass that was dark on the inside. I took a big swallow. My throat tried to cough it up, but I just clamped my lips tight and made small motions with my tongue. The drink stayed down.

"It's good wine," she said. "What are you, a sophomore now?"

"Junior."

"So what? No parties? No boyfriend with a car and a plan to get into your pants beside a dark road?"

"No," I said. "I mean, I could, but I don't."

"Why not? You have beautiful hair and a great smile. I bet all the boys run in circles like dogs."

I took another drink. It didn't burn as much this time and I could taste wet wood and cherry in my mouth.

"So?" she said.

My tongue already felt thick and I thought maybe I should push the glass away from me, but I kept swallowing until the glass was almost empty. The fire was soft heat in the background and I felt warm. The woman's voice on the stereo was like a blanket.

"What does your mother say?" Betsy asked.

"She doesn't say anything," I laughed. "She doesn't give a shit."

"Your mother is a very pretty woman," Betsy said. "Sometimes I watch her walk across the driveway and I see her like your father must have seen her. All legs and that small waist, even after two kids at her age. She makes me jealous, I think."

I remembered that once my father took Brett and me fishing, and when we were sitting in the sun on the bank, he tipped his hat back and opened a beer. "I fell in love with your mother when she smiled," he said. "I couldn't stop staring at her lips." I had just dug the heel of my tennis shoe into the dirt so I could scrape out a flat spot to prop my pole up and my dad was quiet while we waited for a bite. I wanted to ask him what my mother's lips felt like. She hadn't kissed me in a long time.

"Sit in front of me," Betsy said.

I moved down from the couch and sat on the floor. She opened her legs and pulled me back against her, so that each thigh was tight against my shoulders. Her jeans were warm and smelled like laundry soap.

She combed my wet hair back from my face. The comb moved in smooth arcs. I could picture the comb pulling tight rows through my hair, like a tractor plowing new fields. I saw the dark trenches and felt the tines of the comb scrape against my scalp.

"I love the way this feels," I said.

Betsy pulled the comb tighter through my hair. I could feel the pressure build from my forehead to my neck. My skin was cold when the hair fell against it. I took another drink and Betsy held me tighter in her thighs. When she bent close to talk to me, I could feel her breath in my ear.

"Do you want braids?" she asked.

I let my head fall back until it rested in the V of her thighs, where I could feel the rough run of her zipper against the back of my head.

"You have beautiful hair, you know?" she said.

I could remember school days when my mother brushed my hair out for me; even when we were late for the bus, time would stop for those few minutes when my mother sat me in front of her and took the tangles out. I would close my eyes and smell her hands on my head, peach lotion, and it would stay with me all day in school, the brush strokes and lotion, the tug of my hair.

I let my neck relax and the comb pulled me up and out of myself. I felt my head go first, then my stomach and then my legs. I was above us, watching Betsy comb my hair into four sections.

I stretched out my fingers and watched myself touch Betsy, watched my fingers pull and knot in her straight black hair, watched me pull plastic buttons through holes so that her shirt fell open on both sides. I knew there would not be a bra, her nipples would be dark, I would smell grass after a rain.

When Husso walked in the front door, I was next to Betsy on the couch, my shirt was pushed up and my bra was unhooked. My breasts were loose in Betsy's hand.

"Women," Husso said.

Betsy's hand slid free. I could feel its heat leave.

"Hey, baby," Betsy said.

Husso turned the volume down on the music and blew two of the candles out. He kneeled down in front of the couch and put his hand on my leg. Betsy reached out with her free hand and brushed his hair from his forehead.

"Why don't you go to bed and wait for me," she said. "Jaycee is tired."

I pushed my shirt down and sat up. Husso took his hand off my leg. Everything in the house spun sharply to the right and then settled in a slant.

"I have to go," I said.

I opened the door and the cold air outside slapped against my cheeks. The lights were on in my house. My shirt stuck against my back where my hair was still wet. Betsy followed me to the door.

"I didn't finish your hair," she said. She reached out and tucked my hair behind my ear. I could see her breath. "When I have a daughter, I hope she's like you." From behind her I could see Husso in the doorway to the small back room. He pulled his shirt over his head and dropped his hands to the button on his jeans.

Brett's sleeping bag was spread out on my floor when I got

inside. I could see a light coming out of my parents' room. My parents' voices were low and sharp. I closed my door.

I stripped down to my panties and changed into a dry shirt. The sheets were cold and I moved my legs beneath the covers until the heat rose up and I could close my eyes. Everything tried to spin for a minute, but I took three quick breaths and the spin slowed to a stop.

"Jaycee?"

My mouth felt tired and I didn't want to talk to Brett now.

"I'm cold."

"So get a blanket."

"But I'm too cold," he said.

"Brett, I think I'm drunk and I'm too tired to deal with you. What do you want?"

"You're drunk?"

"I'm tired and my sheets are cold and I just want to sleep. Your sleeping bag is flannel. Go to sleep."

I heard him turn over, the soft sound of nylon rubbed against the carpet. "Jaycee, can I get in bed with you?"

"Brett. I'm tired. Get a blanket."

"I'll go to sleep. I promise."

I could feel my sheets heating up against my skin and I could picture Brett against the carpet with the cold coming up through the floorboards.

"You have to get a blanket tomorrow," I said.

Brett stood up and I could see the bright white of his underwear against his skin. Everything else was dark. I moved over and I felt him sink into the bed. He pulled the covers in his direction and I turned over and faced the wall. Brett was warm and I could smell Ivory soap.

"Jaycee, do you think Mom and Dad will get a divorce?"

Outside I could hear wind spit rain against the window. I tried to listen for other voices, the sound of fighting, but there was nothing. I felt the bed settle and the covers shift. Brett's breathing was deep and slow. I turned toward him in the dark and pushed my head against his shoulder. "I think we would stay with Dad," I said.

I put my arm over Brett's chest and pulled him toward me so that he rolled on his side. His skin was hard over the places where the muscles went tight. I touched my fingertips to his face and felt the curve of his jaw, his chin, the small groove below his lips. I brushed his hair back from the side of his face. I hugged him close to me, and under his skin, buried beneath the soap, I could smell alfalfa and grain. I slid higher on the bed so that my head brushed the wall and I lifted my T-shirt against him. His skin was warm like a fever against me. I guided his head toward me, kept my hand firm in his thick hair until I could feel his nose touch my chest. I adjusted the weight of my body and steered his head until his lips were over my breast and I could feel the wetness of his mouth and breath. He opened his lips around me and I could feel the pressure and something pull high and drop in my chest.

The wind shook the windowpanes and the rain fell in a sheet on the house. I hoped there would be lightning and thunder, but for now there was only the rain in the dark, and the sound of something underneath, footsteps or voices. I wasn't sure which.

THE SKIN FROM
THE MUSCLE

There are two things I remember about that day. One was seeing Paul Spence gut-shot in the back of Sonny Green's pickup, and all the blood and that dark pool of something else, something ropey, that spilled off to the side when my father undid the tarp Sonny had wrapped him in to take a look, let's just see what we're working with here. The second thing was how it had been so dark in the morning while we stood around in the parking lot of the Royal Cafe waiting to hunt, and then the call over the CB and Sonny's pickup spitting gravel as he turned off the road. We were all standing there, shuffling our boots back and forth and knocking our gloved hands together, and there was so much stillness that I could hear the pickup coming from what seemed like miles away, and we were all staring into nothingness, black and cold. Then the rain. The first raindrops so small that they barely darkened the ground, and then the fatter ones coming all at once, the ones that would run mud from the road to the rocks, turn parked cars into shapes behind sheets before the day was half over. As I stood in the doorway to our house, thinking about the morning and how the rain had washed the blood out of the bed of the pickup while Paul was moaning, I watched the storm spill from the sky like water from a bucket. Everything beyond the fence line was wet gray and thunder, and I could hear nothing else at all. I thought maybe I would run hot water in the sink and take the time to shave. Aaron Cruz told me that the more you ran a razor across your face, the more the hair would grow, and I wanted something more than peach fuzz under my nose.

The first knock at the door made me turn my head, but I thought it was the wind and I went back to watching the percolator bubble the coffee. My mother had taken the Mr. Coffee and we were left with the tin pot from the camping box. The sound came again and I unlatched the door. There were two women on the porch, both of them in hunter orange and red flannel, both of them dripping water.

"Sorry to bother you, but we was wondering if maybe we could use your phone." The one who stepped forward and spoke was larger than the other one, maybe a good ten years older, but not old enough to be the mother between the two. There were fine lines around her eyes and a small bruise high on her cheekbone. She did not smile when she spoke. "Road's washed out about two miles up and we've got a bum tire and no spare."

I pulled the door wide and let them both step in. They stomped their boots and pulled off their outer layers to keep the water off the floor. I walked into the hallway and found a couple of towels.

"The phone's in the kitchen," I said.

The older one, the one with the lines and the heavy body, followed me into the kitchen while the younger one stood in the entryway and toweled her hair dry. She was blond, with cheeks that were blotched pink like a fresh slap that ran along her jawbone in a line.

The older one jiggled the receiver and hit the cut-off button a few times before finally setting the phone back in the cradle.

"It's dead," she said.

We stood there, the three of us, while the coffee bubbled in the pot and the rain hit the roof. The older one ran her hands down the thighs of her jeans. Her thighs were wide and the wet denim pulled tight across her skin. The younger one started biting at her thumb.

"You don't happen to have a tire that would fit a 'seventy-nine Chevy, would you?" the older one asked. One side of her face lifted in a smile and the bruise stretched long.

"No, ma'am. No tire around here. Not even a swing."

"*Ma'am?* Did you hear that shit, Lily? He called me *ma'am*. The last time someone called me that they were bagging my groceries and offering me a hand out to the car. Do I look like a ma'am to you?"

I dropped my eyes to the dirty linoleum. When my mother was around she used to brag that we could eat off her floor, but I don't think my father and I had run so much as a broom across it in the five months since she'd left, and I could see hairs and lint, dirt in the corners. I lifted my eyes so they wouldn't follow my gaze down and I'd have to be embarrassed by how we'd let the place go.

"My father always told me to be polite," I said.

"Well, you can drop the 'ma'am,'" she said. "Call me Charlene. This here is Lily." They both stuck their hands out at once and I went in order of size. The large one first, rough and square fingered, then the smaller one, Lily's, softer and the nails filed and polished in a soft pink. My hand began sweating immediately.

"I'm Ray," I said.

"If you want to be polite, you can pour out some cups of that coffee you have on the stove before the caffeine boils right out of it."

"Sure, no problem," I said.

"And maybe you could hit it with something harder if you've got it in the house. If you know what I mean."

I knew what she meant, and I found a half-empty bottle of Black Label in the cupboard above the stove and I poured a shot in three cups and topped it off with the coffee. I passed around the cups and pointed them toward the living room and the couch against the wall.

"Nice place you got here, Ray. You own this?"

I lowered the cup from my lips and smiled. "My father does, actually."

"Really? You look old enough to be out on your own."

I took a long swallow and leaned up against the door frame to make myself look taller. "I'll be out next year. College maybe."

"College, huh? Lily here goes to college. Psych major up at Butte."

Lily had her face over her coffee and was blowing the steam across the dark surface. Her wet hair was limp against her skull and I could see how small she was. She was what my mother used to call fine boned and easy on the eyes, and to me it always sounded like she was a teeth check away from describing a horse up for sale in a corral. My friend Mike used to say, "Fuck the eyes. I just like 'em easy."

"We had a class together," Charlene said. "That's how we met." She took a long swallow of the too-hot coffee and wiped the back of her hand across her mouth. "Man, if this ain't a fucking mess," she said. "We've got about a hundred and eighty pounds of venison rotting on that car right there and not a shit thing to do about it."

I walked to the front window and rubbed the fog off. Outside

I could see a blue Chevy sagging to the front passenger side and a deer slung across the roof. I couldn't count the points on the rack from that distance through the rain, but it was a hell of a lot more than just a fork. I was sure of that.

"Damn, that looks like a nice buck," I said.

"Nice, hell, that's a three-pointer, just shy of four. Dropped that son of a bitch in Jackson Canyon just before the rain became a real mud walk. Had to drag him up the ravine, just the two of us, rope him on the top, and now this. Watch that son of a bitch spoil in a warm rain." She tipped her coffee cup and finished the last swallow. "You got any more of this?" she asked, and extended the cup toward me.

"There's a few sips of coffee in the pot," I said.

"Not the coffee, hon. The stuff that flavors it."

I walked into the kitchen and brought back the bottle and she unscrewed the cap and filled the cup.

"Your dad around?" Charlene asked, and I shook my head.

"There was a hunting accident this morning. He rode in with the guys to help out."

"That's a damn shame. Happens every year, though. Especially in this weather." She tipped up the cup and swallowed fast. "You think he'll be back soon?"

"There might be some trouble. Hard to say." I remembered Sonny Green stepping out of the cab of the pickup and stumbling in the gravel, the beer cans sliding out.

I watched Lily drink her coffee. She took small sips against the rim and I wanted her to say something so I could hear her voice. I bet it was soft and warm, the kind of voice that you could take against your ear for a long time into the night.

"So you go to college?" I asked Lily.

She looked up from her cup and nodded. Charlene stood up and wiped the window so she could look out at the car. "I hit that buck on a run. Dropped it in one shot. Bang, and then bang."

I was close to Charlene and I could smell her, damp denim, pine soap, and mud.

"You got a knife, Ray?" she asked, and something inside of me shifted a little. Maybe it was the Jack in the coffee or the closeness of her smell, but I felt my stomach loosen and sweat broke out on my upper lip.

"Sure, we got knives," I said. If the roads were washed out, my father would be a long time coming home. Without the phones, there was no one to call, no way to find out if he was on his way or if I should maybe take his pickup and meet him somewhere. The window fogged over under my breath and I couldn't see the car anymore.

"Well, let's dress out that buck and save me and Lily some heartache, huh?" Charlene slapped her thigh and the dull thud echoed off the walls.

We pulled on our coats and stepped out on the porch. In the distance the sky lit up against the horizon line and I counted in my head until the thunder hit. Three. Charlene untied the ropes and I helped them shuffle the dead weight from the roof to the porch. I could smell the wet hair, sharper than a dog smell, and I could see a few ticks on its neck, swollen and full. He was wrapped in a blue tarp that had come loose, and for a minute I thought of Paul in the back of Sonny's truck this morning with the tarp pulled tight over him and the rain hitting his face. "You weren't drinking, Sonny, were you?" Louis had asked, and Sonny didn't say anything, just wrung his hands and helped cut the ropes.

I handed Charlene the knife.

"Don't you want to do the honors?" she asked.

The deer's eyes were black and glassy and they watched me while I turned him onto his back and tried to spread his legs. "I haven't ever gutted a deer," I said. I had been hunting before, several times, walked a lot of brush trails and canyons, but I couldn't shoot anything. Most of the time the shooting and the cutting happened while I was dealing out solitaire on the bed of someone's pickup.

"You gotta learn how to gut," Charlene said, and with that she rubbed the knife against the sleeve of her shirt and tested the blade on the edge of her index finger. "Rock and roll," she said.

Lily kneeled down beside me. I wanted her to say something but she just reached out and pulled the back legs wide.

"You start by cutting the penis and testicles to the side," Charlene said. "You gotta grab the penis and testicles and lift them away from the body before you make the cuts, like this," and Charlene pulled the penis to the left and stuck the knife in. "You don't want to go too deep and cut the gut, and you don't just want to whack 'em off, either. It's delicate. It's a practiced touch." I watched the knife go in and out in a sawing motion, but it was gentle, almost tender, like a rhythm. "Bucks are so goddamn dumb. It don't take much to make 'em think there's something out there to fuck, and then they walk right into the crosshairs." The knife paused and Charlene rested back on her heels. She wiped her hand across her forehead.

Lily reached out and touched my hand so that I'd move it higher on the leg and help her pull it wider. Blood oozed out of the cut Charlene had made, and I looked sideways at Lily to see if she was the least bit affected by this, but all I could see was her bare ear and her hair hanging in her face.

Charlene tipped the knife point down and pulled the cut backward. "Now, the anus has to be cut out as well, or as I like to say, you gotta get the asshole out. You gotta go deep on this, carve it out like a pumpkin pie." Charlene circled the anus with the knife and the blood ran on the porch. I tightened my thighs in my jeans. I could hear Charlene breathing hard, like she'd just climbed three flights of stairs and had three more to go. "Just free it away like a ring," Charlene said.

I pulled on the leg I was holding and the deer started to slide on the wet porch. "Not too much," Lily said. Her voice was like a whisper, and I knew if I bent close to her mouth, I would be able to smell the coffee underneath.

"Okay, now I just slide a couple fingers under the skin and lift it off the stomach, and I just follow my fingers with the knife." Charlene pulled the skin up and slid the knife behind her hand like she was cutting paper. "Are you getting this, Ray?"

"I got it."

"We gotta cool out this carcass or all this meat is gonna go to shit. The first thing is the intestines. Spoil a good buck right off, leaking out all that crap. And you don't want to cut the gut. Jesus, no. Talk about fuck your meat right there. The smell will make you want to puke, but the worst part is that you might as well kick the carcass and walk back to camp. Amateur work. You gotta use your fingers to push the gut away from the skin, get the skin off the muscle. Take it all the way to the chest bone, get up into the throat and take out the windpipe and all that other breathing stuff."

I could see the ragged edge of bloody skin against the brown hair, and Lily reached out to pull the cut wider. There were dark masses inside, things I couldn't identify, and Charlene just kept cutting away, walking me through it like we were building a model or taking a carburetor apart instead of cutting a deer open on my front porch. Beyond the steps the water puddled, and the rain ran off the roof so that it cut rivulets and ran in a pattern across the dirt driveway. Everything smelled wet and raw.

Lily dug her hands into the open cavity of the deer and I followed her lead. Both of us were red to the wrists and the rib bones were straining beneath us. Charlene cut out the organs and intestines and tossed them to the side so that they dyed the wood porch pink. I stared at the liver, at its size and its darkness, and then I dug my hand into the open deer and helped tear free what was left.

When he was empty, the three of us tipped him up and let the blood drain out. Charlene kicked at it with her boot so that pink splashes fell over the edge of the porch. He was heavy as hell and we had to half prop him against the porch railing. I brought the garden hose up and we hosed the deer out until the water ran clean. Lily got a garbage bag from under the sink and we bagged up the organs. When we were finished, we stood on the porch, all of us breathing hard with blood over the cuffs of our shirts and our hair wet and matted to our faces.

"Now, that's how you handle a deer, Ray," Charlene said. "I'm surprised your daddy didn't teach you anything better, what with the manners."

"I guess I didn't pay much attention," I said.

"Well, your mother'd be proud," Charlene said.

"My mother took off to Montana with a guy who used to fix tractors." I said it before I realized the words were coming out. "We haven't seen her in five months."

Charlene pulled a pack of cigarettes out of her shirt pocket and knocked one to the top. She offered me the pack and I held up my hand but thanked her anyway. Lily took a cigarette and Charlene took out a lighter and held the flame. Lily reached out and took Charlene's hand to steady it toward the tip of the cigarette pressed between her lips, and Charlene kept the lighter against the cigarette even after the tobacco and paper began to smolder.

"I guess we should clean up," I said. Lily loosened her grip on Charlene's hand and Charlene brought the lighter to her own cigarette. The smoke from their exhales blew away in the wind.

"You think I could take a shower?" Lily asked, and Charlene looked at her over the smoke.

"There's enough hot water for both of you," I said.

Charlene stepped off the porch and walked out to the car. The front passenger tire was sunk in the mud in the driveway, but it didn't look flat to the rim. She kicked at it with her boot and pulled the passenger-side door open. She reached behind the front seat and pulled out a shotgun.

I could smell the cigarette smoke and I thought of my mother, how she used to stand out on the porch on warm nights and smoke after dinner.

"I don't want to leave this in the car," Charlene said. "I just got it two months ago."

Our house was on thirty acres of land on Creek Bank Road about ten miles out of town. To the west of us was hunting land, the canyons and ravines, the foothills beyond, and east of us our closest neighbor was six miles away. I had never heard a barking dog in all the time we'd lived out here, but I once saw a pair of coyotes come up to the fence line and sniff at the posts. If the road toward town was flooded, there was nobody coming this way, not for a long while.

"My husband used to have a gun like this," Charlene said.

"Remington pump action .30-06. That's why I had to have it."

"He wouldn't let you use his, huh?"

"Oh, I ain't married to him anymore. He died."

Lily flicked her cigarette over the porch railing and I watched the cherry fade and go out without smoke. "I'm sorry he died," I said.

"Don't be," Lily said, and Charlene smiled.

Lily stepped past me toward the front door and Charlene brought the gun in. The blood on my hands was dried and cracked. I could smell it, smell the wet deer on me. I went into the kitchen and turned on the cold water, dumped a palm full of dish detergent into my left hand. The blood loosened and ran down the white porcelain of the sink.

"I'd still like that shower," Lily said. She was so quiet that I hadn't heard her walk across the linoleum, and then suddenly she was behind me. The rain had distorted my sense of hearing. Everything had the volume turned low.

"I'll get you a towel."

Lily reached out and touched my arm. She looked at me and pushed the hair out of her eyes. They were green, with a small circle of yellow around the pupils.

"Maybe you should come in with me," she said.

I took a step back and felt the edge of the sink against my ass. Over Lily's shoulder I could see Charlene in the living room, the shotgun propped up on the edge of the couch and Charlene looking out the fogged window at the rain and the nothingness with the bottle in her hand.

"What about her?" I asked.

"Oh, she won't care. She'll find something to do."

Lily pulled at the sleeve of my shirt and I stood my ground for a minute before I followed her out of the kitchen. My girlfriend had let me get a hand under her bra one night in the front of my father's pickup while the radio played, and then she left me for a nose tackle on the football team. There had been other girls since her, but I'd kept my hands on the steering wheel in front of me. Sometimes I didn't even need my hands at all. We walked into the living room and Charlene didn't look away from the window. "If that phone isn't working, I might want to do something to pass the time," she said. I could hear the glass edge of the bottle knock against her teeth as she took a drink. "You got any playing cards or anything, Ray? Maybe in that cupboard above the stove?"

"You can look around if you want. I think there's a deck in one of the kitchen drawers."

Lily's small hand wrapped tighter in my shirtsleeve. "We're gonna clean up, Charlene," Lily said. "You just stare out the window."

Charlene tipped the bottle toward us like a toast and kicked her feet up on the coffee table in front of her. Her boot knocked a *Field and Stream* onto the floor and she picked it up and started thumbing through the pages.

I had seen a naked woman once before, when I was younger and Corey Lee had a *Playboy* that he'd snuck out of his dad's drawer. We'd all gathered around at the edge of the baseball field during lunch recess and watched Corey flip through the pages. "Look but don't touch," Corey kept saying, and we'd all laughed and talked a lot of shit about how big their tits were. I remember how much I jerked off that night, until I was too sore to do it again, all the time thinking about the women with their hands on their breasts, bent over so that we could all see the dark triangle of hair and the pink underneath.

I watched Lily undress. First the flannel shirt, and then the

T-shirt underneath, a white one, plain Hanes like a boy would wear, and then she was in her bra, shoving her jeans down over her thighs, and I could see her underwear, dark blue and thin over her hips. And then she unhooked her bra and let it fall down her arms so that I could see her breasts, and they were small, but round, and the nipples were hard and dark. Then the underwear rolled down and she was naked in front of me and I was biting at the inside of my cheek so that maybe the pain would keep me limp against my zipper.

"I like the water hot," she said, and she turned the taps so that the water ran into the tub and then she lifted the handle and the shower blew water against the tile. She stepped in and pulled the curtain closed.

I undressed in the steam from the hot water and when I slid past the curtain she was already soapy with her hair lathered and her eyes closed. I reached out and felt the water, took the bar of soap off the rack and rubbed it against my chest. I watched her rinse the shampoo, and when she opened her eyes, she smiled and took the soap from my hands.

"Turn around," she said.

I turned in the small shower and she washed my back all the way to the top of my thighs and then down each leg. When I was covered in soap, she tapped my shoulder so that I turned to face her and she did the front in the same way.

When we were clean she turned off the water and I handed her a towel. She dried off and shook the water from her hair. "You want to lie down for a minute?" she asked.

I gathered up our clothes in one hand and held my towel closed around my waist with the other. I opened the bathroom door and the steam swirled past me into the hallway. Charlene was in the kitchen and I could hear water running in the sink, the sound of pots and pans being shuffled in the cupboards.

"Should I offer her something to eat?" I asked Lily.

"She'll take care of herself."

I walked Lily to my bedroom and shut the door behind us. My bed was unmade and my clothes were piled on the floor. I kicked a trail to the bed and she lay down on the sheets.

"It's cold," she said.

I pulled the comforter up around us and she leaned against me and I could feel her warmth trying to evaporate from her skin. I rubbed my hand against her arm, and she grabbed on to my hand and moved it toward her breasts. If I closed my eyes I could think of my last girlfriend, Carla, and how tight the space was under her bra, how her nipples had hardened under my fingers, how I couldn't tell if she was breathing heavy or singing along to the radio, and I was so damn worried I'd take too long to unhook her bra if she gave me the sign. I was never sure what that sign was. She didn't tell me that night. Maybe she told the nose tackle. I tried to shake the image of her out of my head and put Lily's face over Carla's, but then I saw Lily under the nose tackle, his hands on her breasts.

Lily turned her head toward me and kissed me, and I could taste the cigarette and coffee, but her mouth was wet and soft and I opened my mouth a little so she could get her tongue onto mine. Carla's mouth had been wetter and tasted like mint gum and the Coors I'd taken out of the fridge.

Lily leaned back and I stretched my legs against hers so that our skin was together. She reached down and touched me and I kissed her harder. I could hear the vacuum start in the other room.

Her hands slid from my rib cage to my waist, and she led me

inside of her so that I pushed my chest against her as she moved underneath me. All the sounds ran together—her breathing, the rain on the roof and the water running down the window, the vacuum, my breathing—and I didn't realize I was moaning until I put my mouth against her shoulder and the sound bounced back from her neck, and then the light flashed behind my closed eyes and I thought it was lightning again, the numbers coming in my head automatically, *one two,* and I pushed myself as deep as I could into her so that I didn't have to move anymore. I slid to the side of her and pulled the sheet around us.

The sound of the vacuum stopped in the other room and there was silence except for the rain against the window. I put my hand on Lily's chest and felt it rise and fall. She kissed me on the cheek and bit at my earlobe.

"That was nice," she said. "I wish I had one of Charlene's cigarettes."

Our wet hair made the pillows cold beneath us and I sat up and flipped them over. I wanted to talk to her, tell her how I was watching her from the moment she came in the house, tell her how I'd held my breath when she leaned against me and held the deer's legs wide, but I remembered my mother and how she once told me that men are all the same—"They tell you they love you and then they come. Don't be like that, Ray. Be somebody better, huh?" My mother in her too-tight T-shirt with the sun shining off her hair, a beer in her hand and her bare feet propped up on the coffee table. I was fourteen with a history book under my arm and I'd just handed her a notice about a school dance.

"That's too bad about Charlene's husband," I said.

Lily tucked her arm behind her head and looked toward the window. "I love it when it rains," she said. "I love the sound and the way the sky looks. There's so much to smell, you know. When me and Charlene were out there walking the canyon, I coulda just stayed out there all day. Walked all the way to the next state. I wasn't even looking for a deer. I was just along for the ride."

I ran my hand down her arm, felt the blond hairs rise against my fingers. I moved my hand over to her breasts, ran my thumb over her nipple. I let my index finger trace each of her ribs and then move in a slow circle toward her stomach. There was something rough on her, a jagged line that stretched from the bottom of her ribs to the top of her hips on the right side, and I sat up and pulled the sheet back.

"What the hell is that?" I asked.

"I had my appendix taken out. A long time ago. It was an emergency. I guess I could've died." I ran my finger along the scar line. It was raised and red on the edges. It looked newer than years. It looked more like weeks.

"Charlene's husband was a really mean guy," Lily said. "He had a real bad temper. Used to like to get his drink on and then knock her around the house for a few hours. That type of thing." She was looking out the window again, at the nothingness.

"So you go to college with her?" I asked.

Lily pulled the sheet back over her and I couldn't see the scar anymore. "Something like that," she said.

"How'd her husband die?"

"I don't know really. An accident. Something." She reached down and ran her hand over her stomach.

There was no sound in the other room and I could imagine Charlene sitting in there in the dark, another bottle in her hand, her legs open, her jeans still drying from the rain.

"You think she's okay in there? We should go back," I said.

Lily reached down under the sheet and took me in her hand. Her touch was slow and steady, back and forth, and she didn't let go of me until I rose to my knees above her and we did it again.

When I opened my eyes the light had changed in the room, darker despite the sunless day, and the bed was empty beside me. The sheets were cold. I threw back the covers and sat on the edge of the bed. I reached back to find my jeans and I saw that there was blood on the sheets, two joined circles the size of coffee cup bottoms down in the middle of the bed. I ran my fingers over them and they were dry. I pulled on my jeans and opened the door. The house was empty and quiet. I walked into the living room, my bare feet marking my path. The carpet was clean, raked in the fresh rows of vacuum brushes, and the furniture had been dusted. The magazines were stacked on the edge of the table and the loose papers were in a neat pile. In the kitchen, the dishes were done and drying in the rack, the towel was hung over the stove handle, and the linoleum had been swept and mopped. The house was sharp with Pine Sol lemon and bleach.

There was a Folgers can on the counter and I pulled the lid off. It was empty inside. My father liked to keep emergency money—rainy-day money, he called it—in the can, and when he was drunk he called it a savings account, which used to piss my mother off since she was always worried about not having enough money put away. At last count there was close to eight hundred dollars in that can, more than a house payment, money my father would use when business slowed down in winter weather. There were still a few grains of coffee grounds in the ring at the bottom, but the money was gone.

I wiped the fog from the living-room window and looked out at the driveway. There were tire tracks in the mud but the blue Chevy was gone. I could feel the air coming through the window against my bare chest and I walked back to the bedroom to put on a shirt.

I looked down at the bloodied sheets, and I pulled them free from the mattress, one corner at a time, and rolled them into a tight ball. I slid on my boots and opened the front door. The wind was pushing the rain sideways and the water came in with the cold. The mud pulled and sucked at my boots. I walked the sheets out to the trash can and shoved them inside. My shirt was soaked and stuck to my back. The water ran from the flattened points of hair against my face. I remembered the day my mother left, how I came home from school and her closet was empty and there was a note weighted down by her ashtray on the table. I walked back to the front porch and looked down at the spot where we'd gutted the deer, and if I looked close enough, I could see the bloodstain on the bare boards. I got down on my knees and put my nose to the wood, trying to smell the blood and hair, find the exact spot where insides had spilled over.

PUSH

The black guy in the orange hat just got out of Chino. Matt told me this just before we rolled up in front of the house. There were six or seven guys standing on the sidewalk or leaning up against the fender of a car parked in front. The guy in the orange hat was taller than the others, fat, wore wraparound sunglasses, and kept pulling at a 40 from a brown paper bag.

"Keep your head down and don't look at them," Matt told me. "They see you watching them from the car and they're gonna think we're running some game on them. I don't have to tell you what that means." Matt said this all in one breath and then he was out of the car and crossing to their side of the street.

I cracked my window and pulled my cigarettes from my front pocket. With the gap in the window I could hear the radio from the car across the street, a spatter of voices, and then the bass shaking the windows. I couldn't hear anything else, not even the sound of Matt's tennis shoes kicking a beer can as he crossed back over, and then the driver's-side door swung open in a warm breath of South Central air and Matt jumped in the seat. It was December, seventy degrees and eleven A.M.

"Done, done, done," Matt chanted. He beat an open palm against the steering wheel as he started the car and pulled into the street without looking over his shoulder. I didn't even know why he came into this neighborhood to score, but Matt said there was no way he was gonna buy dope from some Border Brother standing on a street corner downtown. He said those Mexicans shoved the dope up their asses to get it into the States. These black guys were all two steps from prison and none of them were eager to have anything up their ass. They might cut their dope with crayons, but you could see that right away. You weren't guessing how many times the dope had been stepped on, or who had rear-ended it last.

"Did you see that big son of a bitch?" Matt asked. "I think I held my breath when I walked by him. Fried-food-eatin' brother. I'll tell you that much."

Matt was talking this morning, which meant he wasn't sick and just trying to guide the car north toward Barnsdall Park so he could fix. I'd been with him on a sick day before, and he had made me slide over into the driver's seat even though I didn't have my license. He was bent double with stomach cramps, stomping his feet hard on the floorboards, and every time he breathed snot ran out of his nose. I couldn't even look at him. I just smoked and drove until he told me the cigarette made him sick, and if I didn't floorboard the gas pedal, he was going to take a tire iron to me.

He rolled his window down and drove without talking, north past the west hundred streets, then west toward South Vermont. Matt didn't like to take the freeways back, said he couldn't stand the waiting or the smell. He would rather drive the stop-and-go route of South Vermont through the chain-linked neighborhoods until we hit the east side of Hollywood. He liked the way the houses changed, the corner stores with the neighborhood kids out front finally ebbing out in one long Pacific wave to stores with glass fronts and gold trim as North Vermont crossed into Beverly Hills. It was a long time before the scene changed, and for mile after mile we would get the hard stares from nappy-haired kids on bikes, tank-topped guys leaning on cars, bandannas with beer bottles.

I turned my head to watch two fenced pit bulls fight. One was on a leash and the guy leading him just stood there watching while his dog took the other one by the neck.

"I got the solution, David," Matt said. My mother had named Matt after our father, and I was named after a guy she once liked in high school. We were both named after men we never knew. "I saw it all today and it was clear as a fuckin' bell."

Lunch period would be starting soon at school. We still had an open high-school campus and most people would filter out and not come back for fifth period. I kept thinking I might make it to school today, but Matt was my ride and he'd skipped out after lunch when he was seventeen and just decided not to go back. He was working in a tattoo place in West Hollywood, but they didn't open until after noon and he needed the dope to calm his hands. He couldn't tattoo naked chicks gripping lightning bolts with their thighs if he was dope sick and miles from his connection.

"You saw those guys out front today, right?" Matt turned the radio off and shook out another cigarette. He was wearing a black T-shirt and his arms were bare below the biceps. I could see the skip of needle marks running a track inside his left arm. His veins stood out like buggy whips.

"I saw the guy from Chino. He's the only one I paid attention to," I said. We drove by a couple of black girls in short skirts. All the girls down here were strawberry girls, willing to fuck or suck for some crack or money to buy it. Crack was what everybody had switched to, except the white kids from the Valley, and the ones who came through downtown. Crack was the new diamond, mined right out of ghetto kitchens. We had to go a lot deeper into the neighborhoods to find heroin anymore.

"That connect up in the house is his mother. Two of those other guys are her kids, too. Can you believe that shit? She's like in her fifties, weighs maybe a buck-o-eight, and she's the one selling the dope up there. Josephine. Fuckin' old Josephine. Anyway, I've been working her a little, you know. Getting on her good side, kissing her ass. I know I'm making progress 'cause she's weighing my half gram way over."

If anyone could charm some woman dealer, it was Matt. He was just one of those guys who looked better on dope. He was smooth and people tended to trust him a lot more than they should. His buddy, TJ, had tattooed both of Matt's arms from wrist to shoulder, and he kept his hair jet black even though we were blond boys in our baby pictures. He had eyes that said either he was genuine or he might shoot you and not much care, but his smile didn't often flinch. Even the black guys in the neighborhoods brought him in and let him come around. Matt said it was because he had money and never questioned the rules.

"I go in there today and it's business as usual. She's running shop, you know, and the phone is ringing and she usually goes into this room with the door shut and comes back with the stuff. But this time she tells me to follow her and she takes me into the room. It's a bedroom, just a bed and a dresser, nothing else, and she opens the dresser drawer and it's full of dope. I don't know what the fuck it's all about, right? Like is she showing off or just bombed out of her skull. I'm not even kidding. Full of dope. Some of it's already wrapped and weighed out, and the rest is right there in Ziplocs. So she weighs out the stuff herself, even though I know she's already got some weighed in the drawer, but she's making it heavy, like I said, and I'm all fuckin' smiles when I give her the money, right, like your secret is safe with me." Matt laughed.

I rolled my window down and breathed in the air. Sometimes the air here smelled like gasoline and oil and was thick as frosting that had been spread through the sky. Other times the air was so clear that I could smell the flowers at Rosedale Cemetery as we drove by.

"Are you listening to me, David, or what? This is the part, man." Matt didn't wait for my answer, couldn't stand to pause this long in the telling. "I saw where she keeps the money."

Some of the houses had their Christmas lights up and I could see them waving from the roof edges. It was funny how Christmas lights looked so bad on houses during the day, kind of cheap and lonely, but then at night they cut out sharp images of trees, garage angles, bushes, and windows. They added an edge to the night, made you turn your head and crane your neck for one last look of green and red and white hanging from some rain gutter. They traced out things that you might otherwise not see.

"You saw where she keeps the money," I said.

"Jesus, David, I wonder if you're not half out of it sometimes. I mean, for someone who doesn't do drugs, you sure as hell don't have a good fuckin' grip on reality."

I didn't even smoke pot. I couldn't stand to look at everyone and think they were looking back at me.

"What's your point, Matt?" I said.

"My point is that I saw where she keeps the money. All that dope. All that money. She's got it all right there in that bedroom. It's all we need, David."

For the past year, the only beat that kept drumming in Matt's head was the beat that said *out*, and it was an infectious groove that had swept me up as well. The city limits around us had gone electric, kept us fenced in so that we could not journey beyond L.A. County. Matt couldn't kick dope in L.A. He said everything was a sickness and the dope was what kept him well. He wanted to move to Arizona, to Oregon, to Nevada. He wanted a state that was a different shape than California. He wanted off streets with Spanish names.

We had to stop by home before Matt went to work. When we were kids, we had lived in Minnesota. There were pictures of us standing in the snow, but I couldn't remember what it felt like. Our mom lived at home with her parents, but then the job market fell out and she realized she couldn't raise two kids on a secretary's salary, especially if she wanted to raise them outside of her parents' home. She had never married our father. They had been on again and off again just when the sixties clicked into the seventies and Mom claimed that no one was really thinking much about the future. There was Vietnam. Matt and me were two years apart and our father had dropped out of college, gone to Los Angeles to start a band. By then it was the seventies and Mom had a car in her name and some money that her dad had given her. She drove us out to California, to Los Angeles, and planted us in an apartment between some freeways. Our father never surfaced.

"I'm out of cigarettes," I told Matt. I tended to smoke twice as much as him and I knew he'd be irritated that we had to stop.

We weren't far from the USC campus. Matt always drove slowly when we passed the school. He knew a girl who went there. She had dumped Matt months ago, after it became clear that he was not the kind of boy she wanted to bring home to Malibu.

He pulled west off South Vermont and we found a corner store within a few blocks. The outside of the building was tagged in orange and brown spray paint. Matt pulled into the alley that ran behind the store and a row of apartment buildings. The Dumpsters spilled split bags of garbage onto the asphalt.

Matt turned the radio back on and I opened my door. I took four steps toward the sidewalk when I saw the guy lying near the cement wall dividing the alley from the back apartment parking lot.

"Matt, get out here," I yelled.

The guy had his head bent backward and his mouth was wide open. His lips were pale blue. One eye trailed off toward the left while the other one looked straight ahead.

"What the fuck," Matt said. He stood over the guy and kind of pushed him with his tennis shoe. "Dead?"

I didn't want to touch the guy. "I don't know," I said.

Matt pulled back with his foot and let it fly like he was punting a football out of deep territory. His tennis shoe made a dull whack against the guy's rib cage. The guy didn't move. His black sweater scraped against the stucco wall and he slumped to the left.

"Dead," Matt said. "Poor bastard."

I just stood there looking down at the dead guy. He looked like any other middle-aged Dumpster diver, dressed bad and with dirt on the bare parts of his scalp that shone pale under his thin hair. His legs were out in front of him. He was wearing green work pants without socks and one of his pants legs was pulled up so we could see the bare, white leg underneath. A line of ants cut a trail through his leg hair and came down the other side. They were after a McDonald's wrapper with a half-eaten cheese-burger inside.

"Help me roll him," Matt said. He bent over and looked at the dead guy. One of the guy's sleeves was rolled up and he had a belt the same color as his sweater around his upper arm. I hadn't seen it before. "OD," Matt said.

There wasn't a trace of dope or a needle anywhere around him. Either someone had shuffled him out of one of the surrounding apartments so they wouldn't have to deal with the body, or he'd shot up back here and someone had walked by, pulled the needle out of his arm, and used the rest for himself.

The guy really was dead weight, all of it settled close to the cement, spread out and cold. He wouldn't be able to burn dew off the grass if he'd been dumped in the park. I sucked in my breath, got both my hands under him and rolled him up just enough to get momentum, and then pushed him over. He stuck halfway, but I could finger the lump of wallet out of his back pocket. It was a brown flip-over with a divider down the middle. No cash. A Medi-Cal ID card without a picture. Dead white guy.

"Nothing," I said to Matt. "He's got an all-day bus pass. Two days old."

"Sounds about right," Matt said. "Two days ago was the first. Welfare Christmas once a month. Probably got his check and put it right up his arm. Dumb bastard."

All the sound in the alley ran together—kids crying, televisions behind curtains, stereos wavering in and out. The air was thick with food burning and garbage, all of it reduced to the sharp smell of fish. We let his body roll back against the wall and Matt felt into the dead guy's front pockets. "Cigarettes, David." There was almost a full pack of Camels. Matt tossed them to me and we went back to the car. The dead guy saved me almost four bucks.

Mom had bounced us around the city in apartments. We had moved closer to downtown and then farther away, depending on her current relationship. She moved to escape men. She moved to find them. We had moved ten times in four years.

She worked swing shift and was awake when we came through the door. It was her day off and she was sitting in front of the television with her cigarettes and water glass full of drink.

"My boys," she said. "Come here and let me see you."

Her nightgown was hanging off one shoulder and the television was too loud. Matt turned it down but did not sit beside her. She smiled up at us and I saw her cigarette was burned down to the filter, the ash too long.

"You're gonna burn yourself," I said. I took the cigarette from between her fingers, took the last drag, and pushed it out in the ashtray.

"Always my good boy, aren't you, David?" She said. Her words were soft around the edges, like her mouth couldn't make the shape. I wondered how long she had been drinking this morning. "Not like my Matty. Matty has always been the tough one." She pulled at Matt and he tried to jerk away from her, but she wrapped both of her arms around his waist and pulled him down on her lap. She was almost covered by his size. She pushed the hair out of his face and started to rub her hands under his T-shirt.

"Knock it off, " Matt said to her.

"My man of the house. Always my man of the house."

Matt tried to pull away from her, but she was kissing at his back. "I count on you, Matt," she said.

He pushed her backward with his elbows, hard enough to shake the couch and spill her drink on the table.

"I'm not fuckin' fifteen anymore," Matt said as he got his feet underneath him and went into the bedroom.

I got a dish towel from the kitchen and started soaking up the table. I wiped off the magazines and put them on the carpet.

"I'll get you another drink, Mom," I said.

"Don't. Just leave it." She closed her eyes and waved me away. "Why don't you just go to school. Both of you."

I left the wet dish towel on the table. Matt and I shared a room, always had, and he was lying on the bed with his feet crossed and his hands behind his head.

"You shouldn't have done that, Matt," I said. "You made Mom upset."

"Fuck her, David," Matt said. "You don't know shit, so why don't you shut up and quit while you're ahead. *I'll get you another drink, Mom.* Jesus, do you hear yourself? Do you know how you sound? You don't know shit."

I knew some things, but I didn't say this to Matt. I knew about fifteen. I had only pretended to be asleep.

"You gotta see this, David. Check it out. This is the ticket." Matt jumped off the bed and went to the closet. His mood was always like a light switch. "No, no, fuck that. Hold up."

He turned suddenly and pointed his finger at me. "Get me a glass of water."

The television volume was loud again in the living room, and Mom had another glass in her hand. The spilled one was still sideways on the table. She didn't notice me.

I watched Matt, watched the ritual that made the air smell like burning fingernails and my stomach fold in on itself. When he was finished he was quiet. He opened the closet and took a box down from the shelf. The box was full of baseball cards, none of them worth more than the gum they came with. Underneath the cards was a gun, and Matt pulled it out by the trigger ring.

He didn't say anything at first, just let it dangle from his index finger so that it moved slowly in the light. "This is the fuckin' ticket,

David," Matt whispered. "This is the push. This is how we're gonna make the move."

The blinds in our bedroom were dirty and the sunlight came through at odd angles, worked patterns up the walls. I lit a cigarette and let the light take the smoke.

"You're talking about Josephine," I said.

"Damn straight. Josephine's magic drawer of dope and cash. And then it's good-bye, L.A."

"You're crazy, Matt. That big Chino son of a bitch will take you down without slopping his beer."

"No, no, little brother. That's the whole thing. See, I'm just a dumb-ass white kid with money. I'm just Matt from Hollywood. They won't even see me coming," Matt said. He twirled the gun around his finger and pretended to shoot it from the hip like a quick draw from the movies. "Bang bang," he said. "Fat prison bastard. Don't think I won't."

When Matt was seven he jumped off the roof of our grandparents' house in Minnesota. I don't really remember much of it—my memory is in grainy black-and-white like a cheap film. It jumps over segments of time. Most of what I remember is after, like the hospital waiting room with all the people in the molded plastic chairs and my mom holding Matt in her lap and Matt's cheek cut wide. He is shirtless and my mom is using his T-shirt like a rag to soak up the blood. My mother thought Matt did it because some neighborhood boys who were older egged him on. Matt told me he did it because he never doubted that he couldn't. I was the one who did what I was told. I did what Matt told me.

All the plans were already clear in Matt's mind. In the time it took to drive the stretch of Vermont Street, he had carved his vision from start to end. It had to be today, this afternoon, now, before Josephine re-upped with the supplier, before all of her cash went to dope for tomorrow. I knew me and Matt would leave home sometime—we had talked about it while we lay in bed at night, the glow from our cigarettes the only thing that moved in the darkness—but the picture of us leaving was in that same kind of grainy footage as my memory. I couldn't hold on to the thought, couldn't give it any more substance than the cigarette smoke in the light, but Matt had weaved it all together. The door had opened and Matt wanted both of us to step through.

He told me just to leave my things behind. He wanted to start with everything new. I thought I might miss my mother, but when I stood in the living room, waiting for Matt to get off the phone, I decided there wasn't anything I might miss too much. Mom was asleep. I covered her with a blanket off the back of the couch and turned off the television. We'd been in this apartment for four months and there were still unpacked boxes stacked in a corner of the room. This was how it always was. We never unpacked completely because it would be a waste of time. We would just have to pack it up again. I shook a few cigarettes out of my mother's pack and put them in my jacket pocket. Maybe I wouldn't smoke them.

"Let's do it," Matt said. He came out of the kitchen. We went to the front door and then he crossed back to the couch and bent down. He kissed our mother on the cheek and tucked her hair back behind her ear. Her face seemed to smooth a little and she looked younger than she was. He pulled some money from his jeans and left it wadded on the coffee table.

We took the freeway, the 101 south, so that we could ride above the neighborhoods. Matt played the music too loud, kept coming up too fast on the cars in front of us. The sky had a thin layer of clouds and the sun was straining to come through. I knew the heat of the day had already peaked behind us.

"You won't kill Josephine, will you, Matt?" I asked.

"I don't plan on it," he said. "I don't think it'll come to that. I mean, I told her I'm out. I need another half gram and she'll play it just like this morning. All I have to do is get her out of the room long enough to grab and run. That's it."

"What if her sons are up in the house? What if *he's* up in the house?"

"Then I'll have this on my side." He patted the waistband of his jeans where the outline of the gun pulled under his T-shirt.

"Matt," I said, and I waited until he took his eyes off the pitted asphalt of the 101 and turned them to me. "You aren't going to take the dope, are you?"

"It's all under control," Matt said.

I realized this was neither a yes nor a no, but taillights came up in front of us and Matt braked with the traffic. We heard the sound of sirens behind us and the cars started pulling to the right in their lanes until we were all hugging the reflectors. A highway patrol car went by with an ambulance close behind it, both of them pushing the traffic out of the fast lane so they could take up the median strip.

"I won't miss that and I won't miss that," Matt said, pointing at the cars as they went by. His index finger was pointed straight out and he cocked his thumb above it like the hammer on a gun, snapping it with his exhale of *peew, peew* as the sirens moved ahead. "The first thing we'll do is fish, David. Me and you will get all that shit like you see on TV and we'll park at a lake with fuckin' picnic tables and fire pits and we'll sit there in our lawn chairs and fish. I swear, little brother, that's the first thing me and you will do."

Everything on Diablo Drive was just how we left it. The guy in the orange hat was still fresh out of Chino and the music coming from the car was thumping off the windows of the houses lining the street. Before Matt opened his door he pulled his money from his jeans and pulled a few twenties off the top. The rest he handed to me.

"Shove it down deep in your pocket, David. Keep it close to your dick and you're the only one who can get to it." This was Matt's joke. He threw a few quick rabbit punches into my arm and then he pushed the car door open and stepped out into the street. I watched him cross the street and climb the steps into Josephine's house. None of the guys looked at him as he walked by.

I skipped through a few radio stations and then settled on silence. I cracked my window. Matt hadn't told me what to do. I hadn't thought about it until he was gone, and now I wished I'd asked for a scrap of the plan he had in his head. I didn't know if I should have the car running like in the movies or if I should just sit low in the seat and smoke my last cigarette. I opted for the latter and sank deep into the vinyl.

My eyes were closed and I had my lungs full of the dead guy's Camels when someone knocked hard on the driver's-side window. I jumped up in my seat, but even then I thought it was Matt.

The only thing I saw was white T-shirt. A black hand rose up and knocked three knuckles against the glass. The gold rings punched a hollow sound through the inside of the car.

"Yo, roll the window down." The voice from the hand was deep and smooth.

I leaned across the bench seat and rolled the window down. The black guy in the orange hat bent toward the gap. His wide face filled the opening. His sunglasses reflected a much smaller version of myself back into my face.

"You got a cigarette?" he asked me.

I had smoked the last Camel. I reached into my jacket pocket and took out one of my mother's cigarettes. I handed it to him through the window.

"You got a light?" he asked.

I spun the wheel on my Zippo and leaned across the seat. I could hear the tobacco sputter and the paper catch fire. The black guy stood up and leaned against the door frame. His T-shirt blocked out the street.

He stood like that for a minute, then he leaned down so his face filled the window. I saw a ragged scar across his cheek. His skin was deep black. When he smiled his teeth were white, straight, and clean.

"That your friend up in there?" he asked.

"He's my brother."

He kept his smile. When he breathed out, the car smelled like the living room of our apartment.

"Shhheeiit," he said. He drew the word out like it was part of his exhale, but no smoke came out. He stepped away from the car and crossed the street to where the loose knot of guys was standing. Matt had said that some of them were the Chino guy's brothers. I couldn't hear what they were saying. The Chino guy flicked his cigarette into the street and I watched it—from his fingers to the pavement—and it lay there in the middle of the street smoking.

The music coming from the car cut off suddenly and there wasn't a sound except for a lawn mower far away. The guys went as a group, took the steps two at a time, and then the front door slammed shut. The street was empty except for the cigarette dying on the pavement and me in the car.

I have a picture of Matt from high school. He is standing under an impromptu arch with his girlfriend beside him. His rented tuxedo looks fitted to his body and you can't so much as see a flash of color from under the cuff of his shirt because his skin is free from ink. This is Matt before. His hair is combed back slick with gel. The girl is wearing a spaghetti-strap dress the color of Matt's hair. Her smile is wide and she is looking straight at the camera. She has a red corsage pinned high on her dress and it matches Matt's tie. Matt is looking away, as though something beyond the frame of picture has caught his eyes. His eyes are clear in that picture. This is before the dope.

The noise of the lawn mower was faint with distance, and there wasn't a sound from the house. I could feel Matt's money deep in my pocket. I decided to count to one hundred in my head. At one hundred I would think of the next thing to do.

SECONDS

Tecate tasted like fishing. Three cans in and I was eight months back, sitting on the bank with Rob Kane, both of us like brothers, trying to be the first to take a steelhead out of the flat glass river. He told me that he was thinking about changing his name to Barry Cool after he moved to the city, and I told him it sounded like a Capri Sun flavor and he hit me so hard on the shoulder that I couldn't raise my arm to pull my T-shirt off for days. He would've helped me if I had asked, but that one time was behind us then, and even though he could go back, I never would.

I hadn't bought a fishing license since that day with two handle packs of beer and me and Rob fighting over whether or not PowerBait was better than a spoon on a grub or whether night crawlers would get the job done, and him telling me that he was moving away, Barry Cool in the city, and I could get bent and fuck off if I thought he was lying.

Sometimes I drank while I was driving. I didn't have much else to do. I could bag a six-pack and put some old Skynyrd tape in and just drive out to the fence line between nowhere and someplace. That's why I had the Tecate and the sun shining too bright through the windshield so that I couldn't see. I was crawling down a back road and I thought about that girl that was hit in my old neighborhood, right across from the first set of houses. She was in the crosswalk and the guy said he had the sun in his eyes, never even saw her. She was coming back from the corner store, where she'd blown three bucks on nickel candies. There were miniature peanut butter cups, Bazooka gum, and Jolly Ranchers all over the street. He'd lifted her right out of her Nikes. So much could happen in seconds when the sun was in your eyes, I guess.

My mother was married again and moved into a trailer in Sioux Falls. His name was Paul and he had a tendency to get boils on his forehead. I'd seen the pictures. If it was me, I'd turn my face from the camera, but there were the pictures, him with his arm around my mother and smiling wide open as a pie at whoever was behind the lens. He was red-faced, thin-haired, and had a boil the size of a Kennedy half-dollar on his forehead. There had to be a procedure for that, an ointment or same-day surgery or something. Even a Band-Aid would've made a difference. Maybe I should've respected him for all of his honesty and lack of shame. Maybe I should've respected him because he had his arm around my mother and she was full of lumps, too, but hers were on the inside and he had to wear his like a badge.

I was maybe quitting school. I had an appointment to take my GED and call it good and not go back to those rows of metal lockers and the same old bullshit of who fucked whom, or wasn't fucking, or had never fucked, that made every conversation turn the corner on a lie. If some girl brushed past you in the halls, you could tell your buddies that she'd tried to grab your dick and you'd have her nailed by the weekend, unless she was fat or ugly, and then instead of fucking her, you'd just fuck with her, and that was always worth two days of shits and giggles.

I'd played football and been one of those guys, and I'd ran track for a season and been one of those guys, and once Rob got me a fake ID, I didn't have much reason to be any other guy than who I was, Jerry, with a decent car and a shitty apartment my dad rented for me. I'd been inside one of the hottest girls to cut class in three years, and she'd just looked up at me with candy-apple lips and smeary eyes and said, "This is great, Jerry. It's really tops." And after that, I just kind of slunk out of her and drove home in the half-light of a Sunday morning when the air was thin and smelled wet.

After I read Updike's "A&P" for English class, I got a job at a grocery store. It was past the strip mall, over near the retirement apartments, and not one time did I ever have some girls come in wearing their bikinis and looking for the creamed herring. I hoped they would, so that I could have that moment behind the counter, pull off my apron and say something to Roy Vaughn, the asshole manager who used to hide pennies in the corner of the aisles to see if we were doing a thorough store sweep or not.

All we really had were old people coming in, all of them slow as fuck with the groceries and then the money and then the bitching about the bag being too heavy or that the bread was touching the ketchup and last time that happened, they couldn't make a sandwich because the bread was dented and who the hell can have a ham sandwich on dented bread.

There was only one old lady that I really dug, Mrs. Ruth, who came in with one of those steel gauge carts with the fat wheels, and twice a week she hefted the same item onto the belt—a handle bottle of Carlos Rossi blush. Jug wine, the shittiest headache blend of the bunch, and she went through two a week, needed a refill on Tuesday and Friday. Sometimes I wanted to ask Mrs. Ruth if maybe I could swing by the Pelican Apartments and drink with her. I'd just sit on one of those floral-print couches and let her talk about the Depression or how she had to work during the war and we'd just get tossed and maybe I'd cook her some pasta and light a candle. She always called me Jerry.

Maybe one day that asshole Roy Vaughn would make a scene with her and I'd stand up in her defense, throw my apron onto the checkout stand, and follow her out of the store. Maybe I had been looking for the wrong women all along, the cattle from the cow. It was a housedress over orthopedic shoes and Carlos Rossi that would break my chain.

Pop was home, so I pulled into the driveway and cut the engine. He still kept the one-bedroom trailer my mom had left him in. He hadn't done a thing to it since she'd walked, and the weeds had plotted a slow takeover of the lot. The third step to the porch had broken in the center and the screen door was hanging on by a nail. If I was a better son, I'd come over here on a Saturday and bust my ass to weed and water and paint the front and haul out the slow accumulation of crap that littered the side of the house, but I wasn't a better son. I cashed his checks and came around when I had a buzz and my gas light had kicked on.

I knocked on the door and let myself in. Pop was in his chair in front of the TV, and he turned around at the sound of the door coming open.

"Hey, Pop," I said.

"Jerry. I was hopin' you'd be around today. You bring us something to drink, huh? A little bit of something." He was in a dirty T-shirt and jeans and his hair was all flattened on one side like he'd been sleeping.

"You know you can't drink, Pop. We go through this all the time."

"Aaaahhh, Jerry. It's all bullshit. I haven't had a drink in six months and I'm all good now. What does anybody know."

"What's on the tube?"

"Just some John Wayne movie. I don't know. I can't stand these damn Westerns. They're worse than a soap opera. It's like there's something going on that they all know about and they're not letting the rest of us in on it."

"You got cigarettes?" He tossed me his pack of Camel shorts. "Why don't you find us a game, Pops."

He flipped through the channels, but there was nothing but skinny girls on skates. "Maybe later, huh, Jerry?"

"You eat today?"

"I had eggs this morning."

I walked into the kitchen. There were plates and pans stacked in the sink, all of them stuck with dried food. It smelled like the alley behind the drive-through seafood place Rob used to work at. "You need to do some dishes," I said.

"Hey, Jerry, you want to go out and get us some drink, huh? Maybe a pizza and a bottle. You could stay over and we could just have some drink and play some pinochle."

"I hate pinochle, Pops. It's not a real game."

When I was eight, Pops was one of the best sales recruiters around. He used to wear a suit to work, sharkskin silver, and he had this one tie that had all these green and gold swirls on it. I used to visit his office, over off Antelope, and I could remember the particle-board tables and the coffee stains on the carpet, how the guys he hired would sit in folding chairs while Pops gave his speech about how much money they could make if they followed what he taught them, how they wouldn't make less than a thousand a month, even if they didn't sell a damn thing, and then he'd go for the gut and tell them back when he started he was making five grand a month working part-time and the guys with the bad skin would shake their heads and rub the shine on the tips of their shoes with a licked thumb and the van would pull up out front and they'd load up their Kirby cases and climb in. Pops would scatter them all over town and then he'd wait by the phone for the call—"Let me just call my manager at the office and see if maybe we can get you a discount"—and Pops would take the call and by the end of a fifteen-minute conversation he'd have some housewife committing not only to the Kirby, but to buying the attachments and the extended service contract as well.

He was the best in his region. The big manager came to dinner one time and my mother got a recipe for Harvey Wallbangers from a magazine, and by the time the manager got there, she and Pops were so hammered that they had to call out for Chinese food because my mother burned the roast, and she passed out on the couch with her good dress on, hiked up over her knees. My mother used to be a dancer after high school, and she had long legs with a hard knot of muscle bunched high on her calves. She wore bangs when other mothers had one-length hair, and when she slept her lips would turn down at the corners in a pout. The manager gave Pops a raise the next week. The next month, Pops was driving a brand-new Ford and my mother had quit her job at JCPenney. At Christmas there were train sets and a baseball glove and race cars under the tree, and my mother was wearing a diamond necklace and laughing a lot in the bedroom late at night.

Pops hurt his back the next year, fell off a ladder while he was putting up a banner across the office window, and there were the bottles of pain pills and the vodka chasers and then he couldn't hardly sit in a chair for more than twenty minutes and then there was the Ford wrapped around an oak tree out Red Bank Road and Pops was told that he'd done a really good job for the company, but it was time to hang up his green-and-gold tie and take some time to get healthy again. That was nine years ago. The layers of his life sloughed off like the skin on an onion. First went the second car, then the big house. My mother went back to Penney's, then she went to Sioux Falls and the furniture went and the sharkskin suit withered and faded in the back of the closet.

Pops whistled twice and Smokey came slinking out from behind the TV. The bell on her collar tinkled and she raised herself up to the side of the chair so Pops could lift her onto his lap. She was a ferret Pops won in a poker game from one of his drinking buddies. It wasn't even legal to have her, but she took better care of herself than a dog could, and God knows I couldn't stand a cat. In my opinion, there was nothing worse than a cat rubbing itself against your leg and hauling ass when you reached down to pet it. Cats were the cock teasers of the pet population.

"You talked to your mother lately, Jerry?"

"It's been a few weeks, Pops."

"You should call her and tell her I said hi." I could hear Smokey's bell tinkling while Pops scratched her with a finger under her collar. She stretched out her neck and stared out over the arm of the chair. "We could call her right now, you know. Use my phone."

I watched Pops' finger work around Smokey's neck, and then the slow slide over the curve of her front shoulders and down the long slant of her back. "You want me to make you some pasta, Pops?"

"Come to the city, Jerry," Rob told me. I could hear him exhale into the phone, and I wanted a cigarette so badly that I balanced the phone against my chin and walked the four rooms of the apartment, looking for a butt. I found one that had been rubbed out in a dinner plate in the sink.

"I don't want to move, Rob. What the hell am I gonna do in the city?"

"Same as you do there, stupid. Screw around, work a jerkoff job, and hang out. Drink too much."

"I can't just quit my job." I turned the gas on a stove burner and held the butt down to spark it. "I got my dad here. It would kill him if I left him alone."

"Jerry, Jerry. You're such a pussy. Why don't you just admit that you're scared to do something you've never done?"

"Where would I live, Rob? My car? I don't have the money to put down on anything in the city."

"You can move in with me. Sleep on my couch. I'm never home. And you could have the bed anytime you wanted it. Even if I was home." I heard him laughing and the sound of ice clicking in a glass. "The city can change you, Jerry. You might like it. I just got my hair done. It's all close to my head, you know, sleek, with black tips. It's too fucking much."

I tried to picture Rob with black-tipped hair. He was short and broad at the shoulders with a narrow jaw and front teeth that jumped out when he smiled. "I don't think it's a good time, Rob. Not right now."

"You know what I'm doing, Jerry? It's the best thing. I'm out chasing the bug, Jerry. Bareback rider and everybody wants me now."

"I don't know what you mean."

"See, Jerry? That's exactly what I'm talking about. You're stuck. You could get down here and something good could happen. There's so much I could show you." He laughed again and I heard voices in the background.

"Who's over there?"

"Oh, Jerry, new friends. I have tons of friends you've gotta meet. You'd be very popular. We could chase together, go down like Butch and Sundance. It would be tops, Jerry. You and me could find the needle in the hay."

I dialed her number from memory and I thought I could hear my breathing traveling across the wire, bouncing through the states in between us. I tried to imagine the phone on the other end, what color it was, where it sat in the house. I pictured it as a beige phone, sitting on the bar area in the kitchen. There were probably pens in a coffee cup and stacks of small paper squares with names and numbers on them. *Bob at work 842-6840. Janet called— call her re: Tuesday.*

The phone picked up and a woman answered, not my mother, and I could tell she was older than me, but not by much. "Yes?"

"Is Barbara there?"

There was a silence and then I heard a sound like the phone shifting to the other ear and the woman came back on the line. "Who is this, please?"

"This is Jerry."

"Jerry?" Again the pause.

"Her son. Jerry."

"Oh, God, I'm sorry. *Jerry*, of course." The voice was too relieved to have narrowed me from the pack of other Jerrys that must have called the house regularly.

"Is my mother there?"

"Your mother? Jerry, I thought you knew. I thought someone had called you and told you. I mean, my dad's been so over- whelmed with everything, I just assumed if he didn't, then some- one would. I'm so sorry."

"Who are you? What's going on out there?"

"Hold on, Jerry."

I heard the phone being set on a surface, probably the bar countertop—now I saw it in Formica laminate, fake wood—and even though there was mostly silence, if I held my breath I thought I could hear voices in the background in the distance.

"Jerry?" It was another woman's voice. "We've never met, but I've been good friends with your mother for several years now."

"Can I please talk to my mother?" I was biting at my cuticle on my thumb, and I thought if I sucked hard enough at the skin, I could get some nicotine out since there wasn't so much as a filter in my apartment. My stomach felt greasy.

The woman exhaled hard and I could feel it vibrate through the phone, against my ear. If she had been sitting next to me, the breath in my ear would've surpassed sensual and gone on to kinky. I moved the phone back a little. "Your mother isn't well, Jerry." The woman's voice was shaky. "She's been in the hospital for a while now, and ummm, she's not improving."

"I'm sorry, but I'm not really sure I understand," I said.

"The cancer, Jerry. It just came on her so fast."

"She said she was having those treatments, and the surgery. She told me she was fine."

"Well, she wanted to believe that, Jerry. It was just too far gone for the doctors. They tried everything, but your mother got so sick and now they've just been trying to keep her out of pain."

I almost said, No pain, no gain, but I just ran my hand through my hair instead and sat back on the one chair I owned. "So you're telling me she's dying."

"It's really for the best, Jerry. I hate to be the one to say that, but she doesn't have a life now. The chemo, the hurting and the spreading, and now she can't eat. I know Barbara wouldn't want to be like this."

"I should tell my dad."

"Maybe you could come out here, Jerry. Not now, maybe. There's no reason to see her like this, but there will be a funeral and you'll have to be here. You could make some arrangements?"

I hit the cut-off button on the phone and dropped it on the carpet. I tried to think of my mother, tried to see her in that green dress that she used to wear, with a cocktail glass in her hand, the kind that is wide-mouthed and is always full of some clear drink with a green olive drifting to the side. I tried to picture her when money was flush and there was the midnight laughter and her dancing in the living room to some old 45 and Pops cutting in. I could see it a little, like shadows against the back of my eyelids, and there wasn't color anymore.

On my way to Pops' I drove through town. Past the strip mall, I saw her, Mrs. Ruth with that big-ass metal cart rolling behind her. I knew her from the back, the way her shoulders rolled forward and she kept her shaggy gray head cocked a little to the left. She was probably on her way back from a Carlos Rossi trip. It was Friday, and she'd have drink for the weekend if she could spread it out over the days. She was in a navy housedress, and even though she walked with thick steps, one black shoe in front of the other, I could see myself pulling a blanket up on her couch and telling her everything with my teeth gray from red wine. I thought about slowing down and pulling to the curb, seeing if she needed a lift to the apartments, but I figured with her cart, she could do it on her own. She was used to it. I waved to her, but she didn't see me. My work apron was wadded in the Dumpster behind my apartment.

I stopped at the corner store on my way to Pops' and wrote a check large enough to take my account down to pocket lint and cents. I cracked into the carton of smokes first and a bottle second. Camel on whiskey, cowboy in the desert. I turned the music too loud.

Pops was in his chair, dirty T-shirt and jeans. "Jerry. I was hopin' you'd come around. You bring us something to drink, huh? A little bit of something." There was a game show on television. A skinny girl in a white shirt that said *I love Bob* was spinning the wheel. She looked like she might have a boyfriend in a meth lab somewhere up in the sticks.

"What's good around here, Pops?" I threw him a carton of Camel shorts and sat down on the couch.

"Did you see that sunset, Jerry? It's the goddamn best thing I've seen in six months. You know, they can show you everything on television these days—people fucking and stealing and sticking a needle in their arms. Hell, you can even watch a guy fish and pull a damn wide-mouth out of a dirty river. But they ain't found a way to make the sunset like life, you know? I remember when Ted Turner put color in everything that was all black-and-white and he made the skin too pink and the hair too yellow and all the women looked like whores. But you can't ever capture that kind of sunset. You want to pull a chair out and watch it go down with me?"

"I brought us a little drink, Pops. Something for you and me."

He sat up and smoothed his hair back. "Well, let me get myself a little more presentable, Jerry. You shuffle those chairs out and I'll be right with you."

I got the lawn chairs from behind the dining-room table and set them on the narrow porch, opened them up so their legs spread wide toward the west. I heard water running inside, and I lit up a cigarette with one of those cheap plastic lighters that will always fail you when you need them the most. Pops was right. The sun was sinking slowly on the foothills, and the sky was a color of orange that didn't come in a crayon box. There were green streaks in it, gold on the wake, all of it smeary on the edges.

When Pops came out, he had slicked back his hair and changed his shirt. The jeans were the same ragged-bottom denim he'd been wearing. I could smell '55 T-bird cologne on him, something from way back. I passed the bottle to him, and when he took it, he put his hand on mine for a second, and his hand was warm and soft.

"This is good times, Jerry. It's been too damn long."

"It's Friday, Pops. What else can a couple of guys have going on, huh?"

"Can you see that sunset?"

I held my arm up in front of my eyes and squinted below the sleeve of my shirt. "You could go blind looking at it, don't you think, Pops?"

He had the bottle up and was looking out across the weed-choked yard. "I could get out there and dig that shit up, Jerry. Put in a yard. Maybe me and you could do it when the weather gets good."

"We could rent a rototiller for cheap. Dig it up and start all over again."

The screen door shuddered and the bottom corner lifted up. Smokey had her nose against the metal and she was trying to squeeze through the gap.

"Watch Smokey, Pops. She's right behind you."

Pops turned in his chair and dropped his hand in time to catch Smokey in the middle of her slick belly. He brought her up to his lap and she tried to jump down, but he held her close to his stomach.

"This little son of a bitch is always on me, Jerry. Always pushing me. I love her, though." He started scratching her behind her small ears and she went stiff against him. She stretched out her neck and started staring off toward the driveway. "You know, when I hurt my back, all I wanted was to still have a place around here in this family. A sense of accomplishment. I mean, you and your mother were all I had, all I cared about. And then I was stuck in bed and all that shit happened, and your mom started going to work and I was at home. What could I do? I cleaned that house every day, Jerry, like it was all I was. Your mother came home to dishes in the cupboards, that fucking Kirby still warm, and dinner on the stove. I washed her clothes and made the bed. That's all I was, Jerry. If she didn't notice what I'd done during the day, I'd get so pissed off I wanted to hit a door. We used to fight all the time over that, you know. Me and your mother. Always me needing that pat on the head after the accident." He took a drink from the bottle and opened a pack from the carton beside the chair. I leaned over and gave him a light. He pulled the smoke in and then blew it out so that it hung in the yard and caught the sunset. "Then I just stopped giving a shit, Jerry. I threw in the white towel. I stopped expecting her to care, and as soon as I stopped expecting, she stopped caring and I didn't give a shit what I did during the day. I left piss in the toilet. It's what she expected from me, anyway."

A cricket started fiddling a square-dance number and another one joined in from the west side of the yard. The sun had sunk to a sliver of thumbnail between breasts of hills and I tried to look out at it and see where the color changed, but if I looked too long, I had to close my eyes and see the spots it left behind. There were too many colors that I couldn't define. They just bled together against the clouds.

Pops slid Smokey's collar off. I heard the bell tinkle and go still. He set her down on the warped boards of the porch and scratched her a couple times behind the ears before she slid away from him and jumped over the edge so that she folded down the weeds around her. I sat up in my chair and tried to get my legs under me without making too much noise so I could catch her.

Pops reached out and grabbed my arm. "It's okay, Jerry. She'll be just fine."

We watched her in the yard. She sniffed at the grass, the yellow weeds and sharp star thistle. She lifted a hind leg and scratched herself. For a second she raised up and sniffed the air, then she went down on all fours again and skirted the dead roses so she could dive under the shrubs—we saw the leaves shake— and then she skirted away.

"Shouldn't you call her back, Pops? She can't live out there like that."

Pops crossed his legs on the porch railing and tipped his chair back so that the cheap metal groaned. "You wanna play some pinochle, Jerry?"

He passed the bottle to me, and I took a drink, swallowed so long that I felt my throat burn and I had to cough back a gag. I watched the stretch of grass beyond the bushes, and I thought I saw Smokey for a second, close to the ground and slinking through the yellow weeds. I watched that shadow for as long as I could, until the sun was in my eyes and I couldn't see the yard for seconds at a time.

ROLLING
OVER

The first time I broke a tray of dishes, Dan made me clean the grease trap in the kitchen and I almost puked from the smell that came up from the drain. The other guys stood around and laughed, punched each other on the arms and flicked cigarettes at me so that I had to rub at the burns with grease on my hands and the smell went into my skin—I couldn't shower it away—and the next time I pulled a tray of dishes off the rack, I was careful. And I was careful the time after that. But then I let a dozen soup bowls slide against the cement floor, brown crockery smashed on white, and the kitchen crew started calling me Trap, and the name stuck like the smell. I had the balls to stand up for myself and I could've found another job, but Dan paid us under the table, gave us bonuses, made the servers tip us out. It wasn't a bad job, and sometimes at night I carried the trash out back to the Dumpster, and I'd light a cigarette and look up at the blurred stars in the faded sky. I could take my first breath of air that didn't carry the taste of food, and I felt good inside. I would kick at the broken glass on the asphalt and listen to the sound of cars and laughter and shouts coming from the street. I smoked the cigarette down to the filter, crushed it against the cinder-block building, and wiped my hands on my apron. Sometimes Jeanie came around and I fed her.

That night she was sitting on a milk crate with her back against the wall, balancing the plate of hamburger and French fries across her knees. It was still warm. I could feel the heat coming up from the cement and pulsing off the building in warm waves, and I rolled the sleeves of my T-shirt up while I smoked and watched her eat.

"Next time I'll remember to hold the ketchup," I said. "It's just weird, you know. Everybody loves ketchup. It's mayonnaise nobody wants. Do you ever remember being in, like, junior high and all the disgusting shit somebody'd do in the cafeteria with mayonnaise trying to gross out everybody at your table? Man, it was sick, you know. We'd say it was come or pus or something—whatever was the nastiest." I leaned my back against the building and could feel the heat through my T-shirt. "And the funny thing about it was that I'd act like it didn't bother me, all that gross stuff, and I'd join in, pretending to squeeze it out like a zit, but not one day goes by when I'm eating something with mayonnaise that I don't think about those things and kind of get disgusted. There's no way in hell I can spoon it out of a jar without wanting to gag a little bit."

Jeanie laughed and wiped at the corners of her mouth with the back of her hand. "Junior high was fucking ages ago. We were still hung up on the obvious one, you know, that ketchup is like blood," she said. "We were too scared to actually say that mayonnaise looked like come. But imagine all the sick shit you could do with ketchup at the table. Smear it on a napkin and pull it from your lap. Call it a period."

"That's sick," I said. "Don't tell me any more. You're gonna ruin the next burger I eat."

Jeanie set the plate on the ground and pulled a pack of cigarettes out of her hip pocket. She shook one loose and I leaned in to light it. "You want a Coke or something?" I asked.

"I could do something for you, Trap," she said. "Hell, you give me all this food all the time. It's the only place I know I can go and get a meal for free." She picked at her teeth with the nail on her little finger and wiped her hand on her jeans. "You can't get nothing for free these days."

I leaned back against the wall and tried to dig dried food out from under my nails. I could hear a plane pass overhead, but when I looked up, I couldn't see anything, not even the blink of red lights. "I don't mind giving you food when we close," I said. "Tomorrow I can get you a steak."

A car pulled around to the back parking lot and headlights washed against the building. I held my arm over my eyes to block out the sudden glare, and the driver of the car flashed the brights twice before cutting the engine. Both doors on the car opened and two guys stepped out onto the parking lot.

"What d'ya think of my car?" the driver asked me as he walked toward the back kitchen door. "Two-hundred-fifty horse power. All leather. Power windows." He looked at Jeanie sitting beside me. "Smells like the inside of a girl's panties. Nice and clean." He had a three-inch stub of cigar in his mouth and he talked around it. He kept his eyes on Jeanie. "Dan know you're out here feeding strays? He wouldn't like that shit at all. You start feeding one, and the next thing you know, you've got six or seven slinking around the back door." The other guy, who had a dumb grin, stepped inside and they pulled the door shut behind them.

"What an asshole," I said. Jeanie was looking away, her head turned toward the small dirt hill next to the building. I could see plastic bags, wrappers, and the occasional glint of a bottle tangled in the weeds.

"You better take this in," she said. She picked up the plate and handed it to me. There was still a chunk of uneaten burger on the plate and I could see the jagged cutout where her teeth had taken a bite.

"Don't you want the rest of it?"

"I'm done," she said.

The back door swung open and the light spilled out on the parking lot in an arc. At first I thought it was Dan and I instinctively held the plate close to my apron, but then I saw it was the asshole from the car and I relaxed a little.

"Your name Trap?" he asked.

I nodded.

"Get in here." I turned toward Jeanie, but she was already gathering up her bag and pushing the milk crate away from the wall. I could hear the scrape of plastic over the cement and the sound of her boots grinding in the gravel. "You better take off," the guy yelled toward Jeanie. He pulled the stub of cigar from his mouth and threw it toward her. The throw was short and to the right, and she didn't turn toward the soft sound it made as it hit the asphalt. Tiny sparks flew up from the cherry as it smashed and burned itself out. He held the door wide and I stepped past him so I could put the plate in the sink. I shot it with a jet of hot water and watched the ketchup break up into chunks and slide toward the drain.

It's easy for hands to adjust to temperature—they toughen more than other parts of the body. I remember my baby-sitter used to test my brother's bath with her elbow because she said her hands would lie about the heat of the water. That's how babies get burned. After my first month on the job, I could plunge my hands in and out of scalding water and not notice the difference between the hot wash and cold rinse. The heat didn't bug me anymore. I could keep them wet and soapy and they wouldn't chap. They would just keep their rhythm of washing and rinsing, in and out of the water, pulling the racks, drying, stacking, emptying the racking back onto the shelf. The life cycle of a dinner plate is short. I could do the job without thinking about what I was doing. My hands didn't mind.

I followed the guy through the kitchen. It was still bright and Gerardo had the radio going on the shelf. The radio only picked up two stations, but we didn't mind. Gerardo would sing along in Spanish with whatever came on. "It's not the words," he'd say, "it's the rhythm." The guy from the car walked me through the double doors and out into the restaurant. The chairs were stacked on the tables and the lights were low. The servers were gone for the night, the last of their side work done, the salt and pepper shakers filled, the tips counted. The dumb-grin guy was sitting in a booth with a drink in front of him and the other guy from the car motioned for me to slide in next to him. He sat down after me and I was stuck between them.

"Look, I'll pay for the food I gave her, okay? It was a hamburger, no fries. She didn't have anything to drink." I leaned up and started digging a wad of singles out of my front pocket.

"Who, Jeanie? Fuck her." He pulled another cigar from the inside pocket of his suit jacket and bit the end off. He had a gold ring with a big red stone on his index finger. It caught the light above us and made a prism on the table. "You're doing your charity work out there, feeding her. She ain't worth the burger you gave her."

"You know Jeanie?" I shoved the money back in my pocket.

"Let's just say we've had our time together. You know, rub the bottle and out comes Jeanie, right? Make a wish and all that. Or maybe Jeanie does the rubbing, huh, Trap? That why you're feeding her?"

The dumb-grin guy snorted laughter and took a swallow of his drink. I could hear him chewing ice.

I started to say something but the guy from the car held up his hand. "Nah, fuck her. This is about you." He put a silver lighter up to his cigar and started puffing until the tobacco caught. He exhaled toward the ceiling and the smoke hung low and clumped together under the light.

I shifted my weight on the vinyl seat so that my apron rustled against the table.

"Nervous?"

"I'm not nervous." I rubbed my palms on the thighs of my pants. "I'm just a little pissed off, I guess. I mean, you pull me in here and give me a bunch of shit about a hamburger after you put on a show out back. I could be finishing up my dishes and punching out right now, but instead I'm squeezed into this booth between you two." I could feel heat in my face and I forced myself not to lick at my lips even though they were so dry they felt like I was talking between two sheets of paper. I could see the prism on the table again as the guy from the car reached up and made a fist. My stomach did a quick drop and I winced. He hit the table hard and blew out a big mouthful of smoke.

"Son of a bitch," he laughed. He laughed so hard that he leaned back in the booth and let the ash from his cigar fall onto the carpet. He hit the table over and over again. The guy with the dumb grin kept chewing away on his ice. "Dan was right. You're cool as a fucking cucumber. Cool as the other side of my pillow. You're a fucking straight-shooter bad ass. I fucking love it." He reached out and slapped me on the back. "Oh shit, I'm dying." He wiped tears from the corner of his eyes. The laughter quieted and then died out completely. I could hear the cooler click on under the bar. He cleared his throat twice and pulled some tobacco hairs off the tip of his tongue. "Now we can talk." He slid out from the booth and I could smell his cologne—wood and musk. "Dan," he yelled. "Danny, get in here."

The manager's office door opened and Dan came out. He had black-framed glasses pushed up on his head and his tie was loose and off to the side. He was a little man who wore button-down shirts that could never agree on where to meet down the center. He was often wrinkled, food stained, and sweaty, but likely to hit you upside the head if you didn't follow his directions the first time around.

"Get us a drink over here. For the three of us. What d'ya want, Trap? Bourbon? Scotch on the rocks?"

"I can't drink. I'm not twenty-one," I said, looking at Dan.

Dan ran his hand through his thin hair and the glasses slipped toward the back of his head. He caught them and shoved them into his shirt pocket. "He can't drink. He's underage, Mick. Not in the restaurant, huh?"

"What, do I look like the fucking alcohol licensing board? Am I gonna bust your establishment? C'mon, Danny." He slid back into the booth with the cigar pinched between his front teeth. "Quit being a fucking baby and serve us up some drinks. We're talking business over here. This is a meeting." He reached his hand down to adjust his balls while he shifted on the seat. "So Trap, what'll you have?"

"A beer, I guess. One of those imports on tap."

"You heard him, Danny. Give him a pint. And get Louis another scotch." Louis pushed his glass toward the edge of the table.

"And ice, lots of ice." Louis grinned.

"And get me my usual—the shit off the top shelf, Danny."

Dan went behind the bar and started pouring drinks. Mick leaned back against the booth and jump-started his cigar with three quick puffs. "You smoke, Trap?" he asked.

"Just Camels," I said.

"Those sticks will kill you. You see this . . ." He held the cigar out toward me so that I could see it from end to end. "This is for enjoyment. You don't inhale it, so you don't get the lung cancer. You get nothing but the good taste. You should try it." The smoke from the cigar unpeeled from the end like the skin from an onion, around and around, so that I couldn't escape its smell. It was hard to breathe.

Dan set the drinks in front of us, complete with trivia napkins, and moved toward Louis's side of the booth to slide in. "Hold up, Chief," Mick said. "This is a closed meeting." He held up his hand and motioned for Dan to slide back out.

Dan got his legs underneath him and pushed his weight up. The table tipped and the drinks sloshed onto the wood. "What about my share? You said there'd be a cut, like always. I do you guys right and you do me right, right?" He sounded weak, like the last of the air leaking from a balloon.

"Don't we always come through for you, Danny? Jesus, you worry too much. You start getting your panties in a bunch and we'll just move on to the next establishment. It's not like you got the best steaks in town."

Dan started wringing his hands and his hair had flopped forward over one eye. One of his shirttails was stuck in his back pocket. "I'm sorry, Mick. I just plan on that, you know. I got kids."

Mick waved his hand like he was shooing away early-evening mosquitoes. "Okay, okay, no harm no foul, Danny." Dan retreated to the office and clicked the lock. Mick drummed his fingers against the edge of the table. I could see the thin line of light under the door, and hear the muted sound of Dan's voice like he was talking on the phone.

"Probably had to blab it all to his dumb wife," Mick said. "She's sweet as hell, don't get me wrong. Cooks a sausage red sauce with whole peppers like nobody's fuckin' business. Slices the garlic so thin it melts before it hits the bottom of the pan. But she's dumber than a bag of hammers, I'll tell you that much. Anyway, fuck them. Here's to you," Mick said. He raised his glass and Louis followed. "C'mon, Trap. This is your toast. Get your mug in the air."

I lifted my pint. The glass was cold and wet. We knocked our drinks together. "You like money, Trap?" Mick asked.

I swallowed my beer and set my glass on the table. "Who doesn't?" I said.

"Exactly." Mick squinted at me through his cigar smoke. "So here's what I'm gonna ask of you. A colleague of mine is gonna drop off a box for you, a small box, a package of sorts, and you're gonna hang on to it until I can get in here and pick it up from you. Now, you won't know when that'll be, because I don't know when that'll be. It could be that same night. It could be the next day. It might be three days or a week. I don't know." He ran his pinkie around the rim of his glass and licked his finger. "What I'm gonna ask of you is that you keep that package with you all the time. I want it to be the only thing that's on your mind the whole time it's in your possession, you know? When you're at work, I want it right there with you, and when you're at home, I want it sitting on your coffee table, right where you can watch it, and when you go to bed, I want you to hold it like it's a cheerleader with a great set of lips and no teeth. You get what I'm saying here. The box is all you will care about until I tell you not to care about it anymore."

As he finished talking, he punctuated each word with his finger against the table, like he was tapping out a slow Morse code.

I took a few more swallows. My bar napkin was soaked through and I couldn't read the fun fact anymore. All I could see were the words *rabbit* and *liquid soap*. "What's in the box?" I asked.

Mick laughed and hit the table with his palm again. Cigar ash drifted into the water on the table and floated to the top. "This kid is too much, Louis. *What's in the box.* Jesus, you've got real balls, kid. This could be the start of a very lucrative future for you." Louis was digging ice out of his glass with his fingers. "What's that commercial for the candy? You know, the sucker candy? C'mon. How does it go?"

"I don't know which one you're talking about," I said.

"You know, the Tootsie Pop candy. How many licks does it take to get to the center of a Tootsie Pop?"

I'd seen it a million times, the big-headed outline boy, the turtle with no color. "Three," I said.

"Yeah, sure, Trap, that's what Mr. Owl says, but what do they tell you in the end?"

I thought about the commercial and I could see the owl with his tongue wagging against the candy. *One two three.* "I don't know," I said.

"They say, 'The world may never know.' That's the end of the commercial. How many licks does it take to get to the center? The world may never know. And that's just like the package. What's inside the box? The world may never know. Get it?"

"So I can't open it?"

Louis snorted and a small piece of ice hit the table. It melted almost immediately. "Show him what'll happen if he opens the box, Louis."

Louis leaned toward me and started crunching his ice with his mouth open. He grabbed my shoulder and put his mouth next to my ear. I could hear the ice crack. I tried to shrug my shoulder against my ear but his grip locked me upright. He let go of me and moved back to his side of the booth.

"That would be a terrible sound if it was coming from inside your head, don't you think?" Mick said.

"So I just get the box and keep the box until you pick it up? That's it?"

"Easier than a ten-dollar whore."

"And what's in it for me?"

"I thought you said you liked money?" Mick said. He blew on the red stone on his ring and rubbed it against the front of his jacket, then held it up so he could look at it against the light.

A no-name guy left me a package through the back kitchen door on Friday night, and that was it. I had the box, a plain brown box, like a paper bag–wrapped shoe box, and it didn't make any noise when I shook it. Nothing shifted around inside. It wasn't particularly heavy, and while I was at work I just stashed it behind the radio on the shelf and tried not to think too much about it, but mostly that was impossible, so I thought about it as much as I could. It was either dope or cash, I figured, because it sure as hell wasn't a spanking new pair of Converse with the laces still wrapped together down at the bright white rubber toe of the shoes. For a while I let myself believe it was shoes, basketball shoes, and I tried to imagine Mick and Louis playing one-on-one down at the school courts—Mick with his suit jacket off and wearing a pair of gray gym shorts while Louis kept calling a time-out so he could dig ice out of his water bottle and chew it and hassle Mick about traveling. I could do it all night—see them on the court—and my hands wouldn't miss a glass or a plate to scrape. In the water, out of the water, racked and stacked. Dope, money, or shoes.

Jeanie didn't come around for a couple of nights and I set steaks aside only to dump them into the milky trash bag and walk them to the Dumpster. I stood outside and looked up at the stars and tried to trace the handle of the Big Dipper, but the streetlights drowned out the connection of dot to dot. I listened for the sound of her boots on the gravel, and once or twice I thought I heard something, but it was only an animal running up the small hillside.

On the third night I put aside another burger and fries, and when I went out with the restroom garbage, Jeanie was on the milk crate, smoking a cigarette. She was pressed so tight to the shadow of the building that at first I didn't see her, almost walked past her and through the kitchen door, but she said "Hey" just loud enough for me to hear it and I jumped before I grabbed the doorknob.

"Where you been?" I asked her.

She had her head tilted away from me—I couldn't see her face, just the glow of her cigarette as she talked to me. "I had some stuff to do," she said. "I got it taken care of."

"You want a burger? I put one out for you. Just in case."

"Nah. I ain't really hungry. I just wanted some company. That's all."

"I can bag it up for you or something. Really, you should have it."

"Can I just stay here and wait until you get off work? Would that be okay?"

"Give me an hour," I said.

When I was done with the last of the dishes, I punched out and carried the box out to the back parking lot. I'd had it for a few days and it didn't bother me so much anymore. I was used to its presence and its weight. I kept thinking that Mick would come around and pick it up, but I hadn't seen him. Maybe what was inside wasn't really that important. I gave Jeanie a bag with the burger and a double handful of limp fries. It was better than nothing. She nodded thanks to me and went back to smoking another cigarette. I slid down against the building so I could sit beside her and pulled out a cigarette of my own.

"It's warm tonight," I said. In the distance I could hear a truck downshifting, the grind of gears as the engine revved and backed off again.

"You busy?" Jeanie asked.

I thought about the walk to my house, the dark living room waiting with the TV that never stopped, my mom on the couch.

"I'm in no hurry," I said.

Jeanie turned toward me and I could see that there was a bruise around her eye and the corner of her lip was split. There was a circular mark on her cheek that was red and raw. I held up on the inhale of my cigarette.

"Jesus," I said. "You get into an accident?"

She smiled and then winced and rubbed at her lip. "Don't make me laugh."

"It looks bad," I said.

"It ain't the worst that I've had."

I moved the box over so I could rest my arm on it.

"What's in the box?" Jeanie asked.

"I don't know," I said.

"You don't know? What is it, some kind of gift?"

"It's a long story."

Jeanie looked at me without blinking. Her cigarette glowed hot and then dimmed.

"Remember those guys in the car that night? The asshole and the other guy? They asked me to come in and that mouthy one, Mick, said one of his buddies was gonna drop off a box for me to hold on to and then he'd come around and pick it up from me. And he'd give me some money for the job. That's it. So I just carry around this box and wait for Mick to pick it up and then I get paid. That's the deal."

"Mick the Mick."

"Yeah, Mick," I said. "So what."

"He's such a fucking fake."

"What do you mean he's a fake? A fake what?"

"Did he go all Italian on you? Mafia guy, like he stepped right out of a fucking Martin Scorsese movie or something?"

I thought about the cigar and the ring, the red sauce and sausage. "Kind of," I said.

"You know he's Irish, right? Runs a dry-cleaning business over off of Koval."

"I don't get it," I said. "What's the point?"

"The point is that he pulls that hit man shit so he can make you feel freaked out and he can fuck you over or set you up for something or whatever sick little thing he wants to pull." She flicked her cigarette toward the parking lot. "Let me see the box."

My chest tightened a little bit and I pulled the box closer. "I promised him I wouldn't let it out of my sight," I said.

"Jesus, you're really being an idiot, you know that?" She took a deep breath and lowered her voice. "Look. You're sitting right here. Just let me hold it for a minute. I promise I won't do anything to it, okay?"

I could feel the rough brown wrapper against my arm. It was cool in the places where it touched my skin. I lifted my arm off the box and pushed it toward her. "Go ahead," I said.

Jeanie picked up the box and shook it back and forth. Nothing moved inside. She held it in one hand and tested its weight. "Not heavy, but not light," she said. "Interesting."

"What's interesting?" I said.

"Could be anything." She shook it a couple more times and set it back on the concrete. "The only way to find out is to open it."

"No way," I said. I pulled the box against me and put my arm around it. "Look, I'm just gonna carry it around and wait for Mick to take it and I'll get my money and the whole thing will be over with. I don't want to start fucking things up."

"How much do you think he'll give you?"

A car went by on the street in front of the restaurant and I could hear music playing. It was old stuff, something my mom used to listen to. "I hadn't really thought about it," I lied. The fact was that I'd already counted the money and spent anywhere from one hundred to one thousand bucks in my head.

"He'll end up not giving you shit," she said. "He'll probably push you up against the wall and have that half-retard brother of his scare you a little bit, maybe show you a gun in his belt or something. That's what you'll get."

"You don't know that."

"I bet whatever's in that box is worth a whole lot more than what he's gonna hand over to you. That's why he picked you. He thinks you're stupid."

I was rubbing my thumb back and forth over the edge of the box and I made myself stop. My cigarette had turned to ash in my right hand and I dropped it to the ground.

"Why do you think you know so much?" I asked.

Jeanie reached out and touched my hand. Her hand was cold

but sweaty, and I could feel the edges of her nails as she wrapped her fingers around mine. "I've got a room over at the Deville," she said. "It's got cable. The bed ain't half bad." Her hand tightened on mine.

I could smell food on my skin and the grease in my hair. The thought of a hot shower and the cool slide into motel sheets sounded good to me. We could watch some shows.

We sat for a while in silence. I listened to crickets on the hillside. Something moved in the shadows near the corner of the building and I tried to track it with my eyes, but I couldn't make out the shape in the darkness. I watched the movement until it passed under a thumbnail of light off the awning and I saw it was a rat, ten feet away, trying to slide his way over to the Dumpster. There was a lot of open asphalt between the building and the fence, and he was trying to figure out the best way to cut the distance without being seen. I pointed him out to Jeanie.

"Keep still," she said. She reached down and picked up a chunk of brick and moved slowly to one knee. The rat sat up on its haunches, licked its paws, and went to work cleaning the back of his head. "Don't move at all," she whispered. The rat stopped, sniffed the air, and started in on a face scrub. Jeanie cocked her arm back and fired all in the same quick motion. At first I couldn't see the chunk of brick, but then the rat rolled and I heard it squeak, high pitched and grating like fingernails down a blackboard, and I heard the brick skip off rocks on the hillside so that a little avalanche slid down to the curb. She'd hit the rat low and rolled him hard, and he was fighting to get back on all fours and run like hell for the bushes, but his ass end was refusing to cooperate. The best he could do was drag himself across the parking lot and scramble for traction.

Jeanie was on her feet and reaching for my hand. "C'mon," she said. She pulled me up and across the short distance to the rat. He was trying to dig his front feet in and move himself faster. I could hear his thin nails hooking into the asphalt. We both stood over the top of him and looked down. There was a small scrape on his back, but other than that he looked fine on the outside. He rolled his front shoulder and showed us his yellow teeth. Even in the weak light, I could tell his teeth were yellow and bucked, sharp enough to cut through plywood and wire. His eyes were bulging from his head like shiny black beads that stopped the light.

"Poor thing," I said. His chest fluttered in and out like hummingbird wings.

Jeanie pushed at his back end with the toe of her boot. "C'mon, little fucker. Run. C'mon, do it." The movement of her boot shifted his hind end sideways, but all he could do was roll without moving forward. "Stupid rat," she said.

I thought maybe I could lift him by his tail and carry him over to the bushes on the hill. At least he would be out of the open and maybe he could drag himself somewhere safe. Maybe it was a temporary injury and all he needed was some time to work the stiffness out. She couldn't have hit him that hard.

Jeanie stomped his head in with the heel of her boot. She just raised her leg and slammed it down and his head was split open and I could see his tongue through the broken pieces of his jaw. Something dark leaked out from under him. Jeanie wiped her boot back and forth against the asphalt. I could hear it scrape over the rocks. I fumbled a cigarette out of my pocket and looked away to light it.

"You wanna take that walk with me?" Jeanie asked. She was inspecting the side of her boot. She wiped it against the ground again, and then she readjusted the bag on her shoulder and walked toward the alley. I jogged over and picked up my box and followed her to the street.

DONNY

It was Donny who brought up eating the dog. We were sitting in my bedroom, listening to music, and we were all drinking beer—it's what Donny brought instead of flowers—and Donny slapped Harley on the back thigh and said that would be the piece he'd take first. Harley wasn't a big dog, but he was part hound and part gut and carried around about seventy pounds of weight. He was long-eared and soft-eyed and liked his days divided into two parts—the hours he slept and the hours he ate.

Tony sat up and lifted one of Harley's front legs. "I'd take the chest. Look at how deep and wide that thing is. Grab that knot right there. That's all muscle."

"That's fat. You'd have to scrape that down and then you'd probably only get a little string," Donny said.

Harley rolled onto his back and showed us his belly and his dick. I hated when he wanted his belly rubbed because of that dick right in the middle. Always in the way. I was afraid I'd take a stroke too long and hit it somehow, and then I'd have to spend the rest of my life worried that I touched my dog's dick and maybe jacked him off a little bit. I had decided a long time ago that the next dog we got would be a girl.

"What part would you take, Nicki?" Donny asked me.

Tony ran a hand down Harley's chest and slapped him near the tail. "She'd take ass."

I reached for another beer out of the carton and kicked at Tony with my tennis shoe. Tony was my younger brother and he had just come home from juvie the week before. He was fourteen and on strict probation. We couldn't keep matches in the house because Tony liked fire. One of our neighbors had lost a shed.

"I'm being serious here. What piece would you take?" Donny said.

"I don't know. I don't want to eat Harley, for chrissake. That's fucking gross. Eating a dog."

"Yeah, but say you were part of that group of people that got lost in the mountains that time—what were they, the something party or Brady Bunch or some shit like that."

"The Donner Party, stupid," I said. I was in U.S. history. I was good at it.

"Okay, okay, the Donner Party, Miss Fucking Class President. The point is that you're there and the wagon is like frozen or broken and you're stuck in the snow, freezing your balls off—"

"She doesn't have balls, Donny," Tony said.

"Fuck, that's not the point. She's freezing her tits off—"

"I think that already happened, man," and Tony reached over to slap hands with Donny. "Give me one of your cigarettes."

They both lit up and I watched the smoke bank against the walls and smother my Zeppelin posters. Harley scooted himself across the carpet and put his head on my thigh. I rubbed his ears and he made his happy noise deep in his throat. I lifted his lip away from his teeth and looked at the long, smooth front tooth. It was hard white like bone. I put my finger against it to test the point. I tried to imagine Harley scraped clean, skull and ribs empty. He licked at my fingers.

Donny exhaled and flicked ash into his empty beer can. "Okay, so you might die, and it's either you eat one of the other dead people who are all stiff and shit, or you eat this dog that's alive, like a cow or something that you can cut into steaks. I mean, would you rather eat a fuckin' *person* or would you rather eat a dog?"

"Maybe I'd just not eat. Maybe I'd rather die," I said.

"Yeah, you say that now with that beer in your hand and the kitchen downstairs, but if you were out there and your stomach was empty, I bet you'd be the first one to ring the dinner bell on Harley."

"I'd eat a person."

Tony and Donny pushed away from me and yelled.

"You're sick," Donny said. "I mean, you could cut that dog loose in the mountains and hunt him like a short deer, gut him out and skin him and put him over the fire. There's nothing wrong with that. I mean, he's just an animal when you get right down to it. He's nothing but a cow that can sit."

We heard the garage door open downstairs and Tony reached over and flipped the switch on the music. There were two reasons why my mom would open my door—music too loud or the dishes not done. As long as those bases were covered, we could keep beers between our thighs and light another cigarette without fanning the smoke toward the window. Most of the time she just changed clothes and left again, anyway. Her new guy was Richard. We'd heard his messages on the machine.

"Your shoes are beat up, little brother," Donny said, and he kicked at Tony's feet. "I've got some Vans at home that are too small for me. Maybe I'll bring 'em over and give them to you."

"Man, that would be cool, Donny." Tony ran his hand through his hair—the same thing that Donny did when he was thinking or trying too hard to pretend that no one was looking at him.

"I'll be right back," Donny said, and he stood up and put his beer can on the speaker.

"Don't talk to my mom, okay?" I said.

"Your mom is fuckin' hot. The last thing I'd want to do is talk to her." He reached down and grabbed the crotch of his jeans.

When Donny was gone, I took a cigarette out of the pack and leaned back to smoke. "I think this is my last cigarette, Tony," I said.

"I'm never gonna stop smoking."

"I want to break up with Donny," I said.

Tony sat up and grabbed my arm. "Why? He's the best. I really like him, Nicki. Don't kick him out of here. Please."

"Why don't you date him, then."

Tony started picking at his shoelaces. He wouldn't look at me.

"I don't know. I was just thinking," I said. Donny did oil changes at Jiffy Lube and I got my car done for free. Maybe I needed him. Part of me was afraid that if I broke up with him now, he'd somehow know about Valerie Cooper, and I didn't want that to happen at all.

I'd spent the night at Valerie Cooper's house and we were lying on the hide-a-bed in her living room with the lights out, talking, and I told her about my dad, about when my dad was on heroin and he was trying to kick but he couldn't. It was a Saturday, and he was crying, and I had never seen him cry, and I could remember that feeling in my stomach, the way it felt like it had narrowed into a fist that wanted to pound its way out from the inside. Tony was little, like six or seven, and I was ten, and Dad was on the couch with a blanket, crying, and Mom was on the phone with someone named Marshall, then we were loaded into the backseat of the car with my dad in the front seat and he kept wiping snot on his shirtsleeve and saying how sorry he was and how this was it, he promised, just this one time and this would be it. I didn't know what it meant, I told Valerie, and I wouldn't know for another year. So my mom parked in front of a house with a broken front window and a little dirty Mexican kid playing on the front porch with a truck with three wheels. Tony kept trying to wave through the window at the kid and I kept telling him to sit down. My mom was back in the car in a few minutes, and I could hear dogs barking from inside the house and I could remember a smell on her when she got back in the car, something that was sharp like burnt fingernails, and she handed my dad something that I couldn't see very well, until he had his sleeve up and his belt around his arm while she drove through the neighborhood and she kept saying, "Stay low, Chris, stay down and make it fast," and my dad didn't talk, even when Tony was leaning over the front seat and saying, "Daddy, what's that? Daddy, what are you doing?" until I grabbed him by the back of the jeans and pulled him flat on the seat. And when my dad finished, he made a noise in his throat and then he leaned forward and threw up on the floor of the car and my mom started yelling at him and Tony started crying, and that's the last car ride I remembered taking with my family—the one downtown when my dad was sick.

After I told Valerie Cooper the story, she scooted closer to me on the bed—I could hear the springs squeak and the sheets rustle underneath her—and she slid one arm under my neck and wrapped her other arm around me and held me against her so tightly that I could feel her heart beating into my back. And she kept whispering into my hair, "I'm sorry, I'm so sorry." I could feel her bare thighs against the back of my legs, and it felt like every curve of hers fit exactly with mine. I pictured us as puzzle pieces, locked perfectly together, and I didn't move, even when my right arm went pins and needles underneath me. I listened to the sound of the clock ticking and didn't fall asleep because I was afraid she'd let go.

Donny pushed the door open and came back in the room. He cranked the dial on the stereo and the music hit the speakers so loud that his beer can started vibrating toward the edge. He caught it before it tipped. "Your mom has left the building," he said. "So what do you say about giving us a little downtime, little brother? Me and Nicki alone."

Tony stood up and stretched. He shot me a dirty look. "Sure, Donny. Whatever you want."

"Put the cigarette out first," I said.

Tony crushed his cigarette out in the ashtray and rubbed his middle finger against his forehead. "Anything else?"

When he was gone, Donny turned the lock on the door and sat down next to me on the bed. Outside I could hear rain and I reached up and slid my window wider. I loved the smell of rain, all the wet dirt, and the sound it made against the fence boards.

Donny put his hand on my thigh and slid it up to the button on my jeans. "What d'ya say?" he said.

I looked at his face and tried my best to look through him. He had dark hair that he kept shaggy so that it fell over his forehead and he had to constantly push it out of his eyes. When I used to love him, I told him that his eyes changed color, sometimes blue and sometimes green, depending on the light. When he was on top of me, I would tell him that, and I would reach up to push his hair back and tell him that his eyes were like the ocean. Now I looked at him and his eyes were just muddy. I could see the stubble on his face and the place on his cheek where he'd picked at his pimples.

"I don't think so," I said. I put my hand on his and moved it back to his leg.

"C'mon, Nicki. Take a few minutes. For us."

"I'm on my period," I lied.

"I don't care about that. You know what they say. I will wade in the red river, I just won't drink from it." His hand went back to my jeans and I could feel his fingers try to wiggle into the space between my thighs. He worked them higher until he was pressing the seam in my crotch. It felt like he was tuning a radio.

"I don't want to, Donny. I don't feel like it." I closed my legs against his hand. He jerked it free and sighed.

"Fine. You don't have to be in the mood, but I am." He dropped his hands to his belt and undid the clasp. He took his left hand and put it behind my head so he could push it down toward his lap.

I pulled away and moved against the head of my bed so that he couldn't reach me. "Not right now, Donny. Fuck. I don't want to leave Tony out there for a long time, okay? Can you just get that into your head?"

"Man, why do you baby him so much, Nicki? He's fuckin' fourteen years old. He has a mother."

"Because if he screws up again, they're gonna send him down to that reform camp in Arizona. Kids *die* down there, Donny. He'll fucking die down there. Look at him. He's small and he couldn't take it. He'd break and they'd kill him." I felt my throat tighten and I tried to swallow, but then I decided that maybe if I cried, Donny would take me seriously and he'd forget about a blow job and we could just go downstairs and have something to eat.

"He just needs to toughen up a little bit. He needs to learn to be a man, not smothered and babied and watched over all the time. When I was six years old, my old man was driving me out to see my grandpa, and he took a big dip of Copenhagen and he saw me watching him, so he handed me the can. Shit, I didn't know what it was about, you know, but I wanted to be just like him, so if he had it, I wanted it.

"I took the can and pinched the tobacco just like he did and I put it in my lip just like him, and then you know what he did? He hit the electric windows and rolled them up. And he told me to hold it. 'Don't fucking spit, Donny,' he said, and I know I must've turned about eight shades of green in the front seat of that Plymouth, but I held that shit in because I didn't have a choice. If I spit, he would've reached over there and beat me upside the head, and if I puked, he would've pulled the car over and beat me by the side of the road. But I tell you one thing, after about five minutes, he rolled the window down and told me it was all right, go ahead and spit it, and I leaned out that window at fifty miles an hour and just hawked a mouthful of spit, and I spit every last grain of that shit out of my mouth until I couldn't suck another drop, but I didn't gag and I didn't cry and afterward, my old man reached over there and patted me on the shoulder like I'd just hit a home run or some shit like that. That toughened me up. That made me a man, you know."

I tried to imagine Donny hanging out the window of a car as a little boy, his shaggy hair blowing into his eyes and him trying to spit without letting his dad down. I almost felt that love come back, but then I thought about Valerie Cooper behind me and how she smelled like strawberry shampoo and I kept taking short, deep breaths to get it all in.

"I get your point," I told Donny, and I slid off the bed and opened my door. Harley was standing on the other side with his tongue hanging out. "I have to feed the dog." Donny rolled over and faced the wall.

Tony was downstairs making a sandwich. "Are you guys done?" he said.

"We were just talking."

"Okay, sure. You'd better not be just talking or he's gonna dump you instead."

"Why do you think you know so much? Why do you have to be in my business?" I reached out and put my arm around him and pulled him toward me. He tried to struggle away, but not very hard, and I kissed his cheek before he was able to rub mayonnaise on my arm and get me off of him. "No matter what happens, Tony, you'll still have me, okay?"

Tony squirted mustard onto the top slice of bread and flipped it over onto the meat and cheese. "Yeah, I know," he said. "Sometimes I just wish it was different."

Donny walked into the kitchen and pulled a beer out of the refrigerator. "Where's my sandwich, man?"

"Oh, you can have this one, Donny. I can make myself another one," Tony said.

Donny put his arm around me. "See, this is what I'm talking about. He's a total pussy. Don't give up your sandwich, Tony. Not ever. You tell me to take a flyin' fuck or whatever, but don't be a doormat. It's your sandwich. You made it and you eat it. Everyone else is on their own. Remember that." Donny took a quick swallow of his beer. "Hey, you guys want to waste some time?"

When Donny got back from his car, we went into the living room and watched him pull things out of his backpack. Inside were a gallon jug of clear liquid, a box of skinny cigars, and a little bag of weed. "A guy at work told me about this after he found out my dad was doing graveyard shifts mopping up at the morgue. He told me if I got this for him, he'd help me unload it and we could split the dough. He said it would be a fuckin' lot of money—like enough to buy that Camaro I want." Donny took out one of the cigars and split it open down the middle, then he scraped the tobacco out onto one of my mom's *Cooking Light* magazines.

"I don't see how a little bag of weed and a jug of vinegar are gonna make you rich, Donny," I said.

"This isn't vinegar," he said.

Outside there was a loud roll of thunder and the lights flickered on and off for a second. "Ooooooooo, spooky," Donny said. He held his fingers up like claws. "We can be mad scientists tonight."

"You want me to get some candles?" Tony asked.

"Nice try," I said.

"I'm just trying to be prepared." He started peeling rubber off the sole of his shoe.

"Anyway, this isn't vinegar. It's embalming fluid. They keep the shit in fifty-five-gallon drums in a room in the morgue. I took my old man some cigarettes one night, and when he went out to cop a smoke, I just siphoned a little off the top and it's just like the songs says, man. Texas tea. Black gold. Just like that."

"You're gonna get high and open a funeral parlor?" I asked.

"Ha, so fuckin' funny that I forgot to laugh."

The rain was pounding the roof. There wasn't the sound of separate raindrops, just a constant sound of water running like the clouds had been tapped and the faucet left wide open over our house.

Donny sprinkled the weed into the empty cigar casing and rolled it into a joint, then he licked it to seal it. When he was done, he unscrewed the jug and tipped it a little to the left so that the liquid came to the top. He dipped the joint into the fluid, held it there for a second, turned it over, and dipped the other end.

"This is what they call wet. Go get your hair dryer, Nicki," he said.

When I brought my hair dryer downstairs, Donny plugged it in and turned it on low. He held the joint up under the hot air. When it was dry, he handed it to me and told me to smell it. I inhaled and jerked my head back. "That smells like shit," I said.

"My buddy at work said it's a sweet high. Like weed, but better. I say we just give it a try. One on the house, no charge. He's gonna unload that bottle for me tomorrow and then it'll be cash in my pocket."

"Okay, so what you're saying is that you just rolled a joint and dipped it in embalming fluid, the stuff they preserve dead bodies with. Am I right on this?" I said.

Donny had the joint squeezed between his lips and he was reaching into his front pocket to fish out his Zippo. "It's just weed and some chemicals, Nicki. Formaldehyde and stuff." He pulled the joint out of his mouth. "I mean, remember that time me and you and Steve Christie huffed that paint thinner in his garage? It's like that, except this is on weed and you smoke it."

"You huffed?" Tony said.

"Yeah, one time, and I totally puked," I said.

"That's because when I said stop you wouldn't listen to me," Donny said. He pulled out his Zippo, ran the wheel, and lit the joint. It smelled like gasoline. "You would've been fine if you would've listened to me."

I remembered when I met Donny. We were at a party and he was out on the patio showing some sophomores how to make a beer bong with a funnel and some tubing. He had already graduated and they soaked him up like a sponge, listening to everything he said, calling him *man,* and trying to outdo each other in front of him. They all wanted what Donny had, whatever it was.

He passed the joint to me and I took it. I took a small hit and it was like inhaling nail polish remover and my lips went numb and I started coughing until I gagged. My eyes were watering and it hurt to breathe. "That is so bad," I said. "I can't stand it."

"No pain, no gain, baby," Donny said, and he hit it again. When he exhaled I watched the smoke tangle around the back of his head and then break away until it stretched across the room. I wanted to reach out and touch it. He passed the joint to Tony.

"No way," I said. I grabbed for Donny's arm. "Not him."

Donny turned away from me and blocked me with his body. He extended his arm out to Tony and Tony took the joint. "Let him go a little bit, Nicki. It'll be good for him. I'll watch him. I swear."

I leaned back against the couch and looked at the ceiling. There was a crease as the two sides came together so that the middle of the ceiling was higher. It had the stuff on it that made it look like cottage cheese, like I could just reach up and scoop it into a bowl with some pineapple slices. I thought about how strange it was that those lumps were called curds, and they were nothing but spoiled milk, and we ate it anyway, something rotten. And then I thought about milk, about how white it was and cold, and how I hadn't drank it since my dad was in the house and he used to make us saltine crackers with milk and sugar on them for breakfast. He called it a treat. "Treat him carefully," I said to Donny, but I wasn't sure if I said it or if the words just formed in my head and bounced around like a walnut. "I'm high," I said. I stood up from the couch and my legs felt like they were far from my body. The feet at the end didn't seem to belong to me. "I'll be right back," I said. No one looked at me. I felt the walnut of words in my head again, bouncing like a Superball, a white Superball, like a cottage cheese curd.

In the bathroom I splashed water on my face and looked at myself in the mirror. My pupils were wide and for a second I couldn't remember what color my eyes really were—maybe they'd been black all my life. Then I remembered that I had green eyes, like my mother, and I smiled and touched my teeth in the mirror. If I looked close enough, I could see the fine hairs on my face, so many of them, and I wondered what it would be like to be a man, to have a mustache or a goatee. If I were a man, then I wouldn't be with Donny because there's no way he'd ever be gay, and maybe I could be Valerie's boyfriend instead. I could see myself sitting at her kitchen table with Mr. and Mrs. Cooper eating chicken, and they were talking to me, asking me about my plans after high school, and I told them that I was going anywhere that Valerie went because I loved her, and Mrs. Cooper reached out and touched my hand and everyone smiled and I kissed Valerie right there at the table, her lips on mine, Dr Pepper lip gloss on my tongue. But when I ran my tongue across my lips, all I could taste was nail polish remover and I spit hard into the sink. I looked at the porcelain and saw Mrs. Cooper's lacquered nails pulling back from my hand, recoiling, because I was Nicki at the table, with my lips on Valerie, and I wasn't a boy at all.

Donny was in the kitchen, running the microwave. I could hear him breathing. It was almost a pant, like Harley after a good run chasing a squirrel up the backyard fence. He jumped when I said his name, and I could see his nostrils flaring in and out. "I am so fuckin' pumped up," he said. He slammed his fist on the countertop. "I feel like I could run a fuckin' three-minute mile. I swear."

"Where's Tony?"

"He's out. He's got headphones on. I only gave him a taste, but it's good for him, you know. Just in case he ends up in Arizona."

"He's not going to Arizona," I said.

"You never know."

The microwave dinged and Donny yanked the door open. Inside was a slab of steak on a Styrofoam tray. Donny grabbed a plate out of the cupboard, sliced the cellophane wrapper with his thumb, and slid the bloody meat onto the plate. It was brown around the edges and there was melted fat mixed with the juice. I thought if I smelled it, I would throw up in the sink.

"You're not gonna eat that, are you?" I said.

Donny started laughing and beat his fists against the counter. "This is for Arizona," he said. He set the plate by the sink and reached for me. His hands were sweaty and it took him two tries to get a grip on my arm. "We didn't finish up earlier," he said.

"No way, Donny. Not now. I don't feel so good. Seriously."

"I'm gonna fuckin' jump out of my skin, Nicki. Just let me go quick, please. I promise it won't take much. Three strokes. I swear. I'm already hard. Look."

I looked down at the crotch of his jeans and could see the bulge in front. His face was red and there was sweat on his upper lip. He was shifting his weight back and forth on his feet, bouncing on his heels.

"Okay," I said.

Donny reached for his belt buckle and Tony walked into the kitchen. "I heard noises," he said.

"Go back in the other room and put the headphones on, little brother," Donny said. "We'll be in there in a minute."

I got up off my knees on the linoleum. "Are you okay, Tony?"

"The room felt like it was shrinking," he said. "I could hear the rain outside and I thought the floor was floating and the storm was coming in." He was sniffling and I could see that he was crying a little bit.

"Go back in there, man," Donny said. "You're just high. It's cool. You'll be fine."

"No. I want to stay with you."

Donny made a fist and started punching it into his free hand. He turned toward Tony. "Look." He lifted the plate of meat off the counter. "Go back in there and then we'll all dig into a little bit of Harley. See what it's like." Donny smiled and shoved the plate toward Tony.

Tony backed up into the refrigerator and knocked the magnets off the front. Coupons and reminders slid to the floor. He started crying harder. I suddenly understood what Donny meant when he said this was for Arizona.

"He's lying, Tony," I said. "He's fucking with you. He's just trying to teach you a lesson."

Tony's eyes were wide and he was wiping snot onto the back of his hand. Donny reached out to touch him and Tony slid away from him along the wall. "Who are you gonna believe, little brother?" he asked.

I whistled for Harley. My lips were shaking and it was hard to get them tight enough to push the air and make a sound.

"He's not coming," Tony said.

Donny was laughing. The sound hurt my head. I didn't think about it first, I just swung out with my shoe and caught him high on his left thigh. I heard the thud of canvas on jeans. Donny fell to one knee and started rubbing at his leg. "Motherfuck," he said.

"Enough," I screamed. "Stoppit." I remembered those sophomore boys at the party, all three of them leaning over the deck puking that night, the empty beer cans around them and the beer bong sitting on a lawn chair. Donny was inside changing the music. He could've stopped at any time.

Tony was bent over with his arms wrapped tight around himself. "It was the firecrackers, the Black Cats I got from Benny Null, and we were messing around and he dared me. I didn't have to, but it was a dare and Harley was lying there, so I just did it . . ."

Donny reached out and this time he got a handful of Tony's shirt before Tony could back away. He tried to pull Tony toward him, but the shirt just stretched and Tony didn't move. "It was just a joke, kid," Donny said. "I was just messing around."

Tony rubbed at his eyes. "I put the firecrackers in Harley's ass, slowly, so he wouldn't wake up, and he just let me do it and I kept flicking the lighter but it wouldn't work. I shook it . . . and still nothing. It wouldn't light and there weren't any matches and Harley finally just got up and went through the dog door to the garage . . . I was gonna light the firecrackers. But I couldn't."

"Donny, let's go get Harley, okay?" I said.

"It was just a steak, man. Just a three-dollar steak." Donny let go of Tony's shirt and stood up. Tony just kept staring at his shoes.

I opened the garage door and walked out into the darkness. Donny flicked the switch and we wandered around in the weak light from the single bulb by the door. The sound of rain was louder in here, and through the door to the side yard I could see the rain under the streetlight and the small rainbow it left behind.

We both called for Harley. I checked his dog bed in the corner and Donny walked outside and whistled toward the backyard. I could hear his shoes on the gravel. I looked in the corner where the dirty laundry was piled, but he wasn't sleeping there. The garage smelled like the oil from my mom's rotting Nova, and I could see the stain on the cement. I had lost my virginity in that car, not with Donny, but with a guy who came to a house party my mom had thrown last year. He was short and smelled like a cedar chest, and he'd followed me out to the garage when I snuck out to smoke. I'd had a lot of vodka and when he was on me, I didn't feel anything inside, not pain or fear. I just stared out the windshield of the car while my head kept knocking into the armrest, and I listened to him tell me how sweet I was. I wondered what Valerie would do if I told her that story in the dark.

"Where's the fuckin' dog?" Donny asked, and for a minute I couldn't remember why we'd come out in the garage in the first place.

"Maybe he's in my room," I said.

When we got back in the kitchen, the light seemed too bright and Tony was gone. I could hear noise upstairs, the sound of water running and then a door slammed.

"I'm gonna go to college next year," I said to Donny. "I'm gonna move away."

He poked at the meat on the plate with his finger and then looked at the blood on his skin. "Whatever."

I dumped the steak into the trash and it made a heavy sound when I dropped it into the garbage can, like something wet but solid, and the bag slid down the sides of the can so that I had to lift it again and pull it back over the top. It was Donny who smelled the smoke first. I was putting the magnets back on the refrigerator one by one with the papers underneath, and then Donny was yelling and taking the stairs two at a time. I could hear Harley barking behind the bathroom door above me, and even though the smoke was only a faint smell, like the smell of a cigarette when someone walks past you on the street, I could smell gasoline and dirt and something underneath that was sweet, like the summer air in the neighborhood before the mosquitoes come out.

WHISTLE
PIG

Travis Barlow told me his plan to rob the fat guy. We were sitting in lawn chairs in his living room, drinking beers and not paying attention to the game on the television. Neither of us gave a shit about the Braves or their chances in the division.

"Go over there, man, just knock on his door and ask to borrow an egg or something. He'll give it to you. He's nothing but nice and polite—the way fat people are, you know, like they know what a fucking burden they are on normal people. The way they take up too much space and eat all the good food at the buffet before you can get in there for the mashed potatoes. Their stink-ass smell of sweat on the bus, like they can't reach all the places to wash," Travis said. "And listen to this shit. One time I was standing at a urinal, taking a piss, and this fat guy is next to me, and I'm no faggot, but I just look over 'cause I have to see. I mean, I figure fat all the way, right? And his fucking dick is like this little tiny thing, like a fucking stem on a balloon, man. I almost laughed right there. They've got fucked-up bodies. They're just wrong, you know?

"I've been over when he was on vacation. Checked out his place. You gotta see it for yourself."

Travis tapped the key ring on his belt with his beer can so that the keys jingled. He was the manager of the apartment complex—twenty units, ten per side, five upstairs and five down. My sister had an upstairs unit, number 4, but she was always across town staying with her boyfriend. My mom and Larry had taken to throwing things at each other and she gave my sister rent money to let me stay out of the house while they "worked things out." I had a good feeling about how they might work things out. Maybe she'd throw something heavy at Larry one night, or something sharp, and I could stop waking up to the low squawk of police radios in the living room. I was supposed to go back to high school in the fall, finish my last year, but everyone seemed to have forgotten about that. I figured that come September, I'd forget about it, too.

"So I'm telling you, I've been in his place and it's like a fucking rat hole, you know, all this shit everywhere, floor to ceiling, smells like a goddamn cage. Nothing worth taking, except maybe his stereo, but there has to be about five or six grand in a shoe box in his closet. I mean, who the hell keeps cash in a fucking box? Anybody that stupid needs to get robbed, and maybe get their ass kicked in the process." Travis drained the last of his beer and tossed the empty over the side of his chair. "He's got plenty of ass to kick, I can tell you that much."

"Why didn't you just take the money when you were over there and he was gone?"

"Think about it, dumb-ass. I use my key, get in, and he comes back and the money is gone. What am I gonna do, break stuff and make a bunch of noise? I needed time to figure it out. Get some kind of cover together."

I had come over to pay the rent last month and Travis had asked me if I wanted to come in and have a beer. He had taken me fishing after that, borrowed a car and drove us down to the delta. I had a picture of us tacked on the wall—both of us in goofy grins under matching Raiders hats he'd bought us when we stopped for beer, both of us holding up fish, my four to his one. He taught me how to gut what I caught, how to slide a knife through the soft white belly from throat to tail and slide a thumb against the inside of the spine until the knot of organs pulled free and spilled out on the dirt.

Travis knew my sister—they had gone to high school together—and that's how he set her up with one of the better places in the complex. She had one near the laundry room and with easy access to street parking. He put her above old Mrs. Santana, who was practically deaf and wouldn't complain about any noise. Travis had been the manager for a year. It gave him a free place to live and the ability to work three nights a week at the Chevron station down the street.

"You gotta go over there and knock on the door, man, I'm telling you. Borrow two eggs. I'm starving." Travis hit me on the arm and knocked me forward out of my chair. "And hand me a beer."

I stood up and got Travis a beer from the refrigerator. "Are you sure about this?" I asked. I could see the fat guy's apartment across the courtyard. The blinds were closed but there were lights in the living room and occasionally a shadow moved across the window like a cloud passing in front of the sun.

"You gotta do it. You'll love it."

Even though it was evening the air was warm as afternoon and most of the apartments around the complex had their windows or doors open to let in the twilight and the cooler air that would follow. There were small clouds of gnats hovering over the sidewalk, and I could smell charcoal and wet grass, the burnt sugar of barbecue sauce on a grill.

I knocked twice and looked back over my shoulder at Travis's apartment. He had his blinds wide open and I could see him in his chair. He raised his beer. I could feel the sweat on the back of my neck and feel the gnats swarm beside my face. I slapped at them and my hand came away with a gritty smear. It was just darkness with legs that could've been anything.

I turned back toward Travis and shrugged my shoulders—no answer—and then I heard a lock turn on the door, the sound of the chain being slid, and then the door opened. I could smell garlic and hear country music in the background.

"Yes?"

He wasn't as fat as I had imagined. From the way Travis lit up, I thought the guy might be nothing but rolls on legs, but he was simply large in the middle, and short, with shaggy brown hair. He was wearing dark framed glasses and a T-shirt that said *Malibu Athletic Club*. Travis would shit over that.

"I'm real sorry to bother you, but I live over in apartment four and I was wondering if I could borrow two eggs."

He looked at me for a minute and then extended his hand. "Nice to meet you. I'm Percy. Percy Morris."

"Josh," I said.

"Are you baking, Josh?"

"It's a little hot out here, but not bad," I said.

Percy laughed and the sound was low and came from far back in his throat. When he smiled his eyes tucked tight with wrinkles at the corners so that the whites disappeared. "I mean with the eggs. Are you using them in a recipe. Baking."

I felt the heat in my cheeks and shoved my hands down in my pockets. "Yeah, baking. Cookies."

"Well, you're a braver man than I. I won't run the oven in the summer. I can't take the suffocation of the heat. Oh, I get the urge to turn it on and put in some brownies or even a casserole, but I won't do it."

Sometimes when people talk there is something about their voice that makes me sleepy. I can feel it inside, in my head, and I can feel myself lulled and wanting them to keep talking—about anything, weather even. Not everyone makes me feel that way, but Percy's voice had that softness to it. I kept staring at him, watching his mouth move and feeling his voice on me like a blanket.

"Well, I'm sure I can spare some eggs for your endeavor. Please." He stepped aside and opened the door wide enough for me to come in. It was cooler inside and the lights were turned low. The brightest light was in the kitchen, where a pot simmered on the stove, throwing steam against the hood.

The walls of his apartment were lined with bookcases, all of them full, and there were books in stacks on the coffee table. He had a couch in the center of the room and a stereo, like Travis said, where country music was turned down low. In front of me was a hallway, and I recognized the floor plan from my sister's apartment. Straight back was the bedroom. There was clutter, but not a dirty kind, and I wasn't sure if his fatness had a smell.

"Nice place you have here," I said.

Percy was bent over at the refrigerator, moving things aside, and in the bright kitchen light I could see that my first impression of him had been wrong. The shadows had made him seem thinner. In this light I could see that he was a large man, all of him wide and thick—even his bare arms were the size of Travis's thigh. Part of me wanted to walk over and plant one of my tennis shoes square in his ass and run like hell for kicks. When he stood up with the egg carton in his hand, I could see that the T-shirt was enormous, and even so it pulled tight over his stomach, the cotton creased in the folds of skin.

"Two eggs you say, Josh," he called from the kitchen.

"That'd be great."

The pot on the stove began to bubble over and I could hear the hiss and spatter. Percy turned the stove dial and pulled the pot to a free burner in one movement. It surprised me that he was smooth and quick despite his size.

"It smells good in here," I said.

"It's just pasta sauce. Something my mother used to make and I improved upon. I've always been a bit of a cooking connoisseur, you could say. Ever since I was a child I was fascinated with all the steps involved in preparing even the simplest of meals. Everything so balanced and measured, and just one excessive moment could ruin it all. There is no room for improvisation really. You must stick to an equation. Salt must balance pepper, fat, and flour, neither too little nor too much. There are rules. You can't just put basil in whatever you're preparing and hope for the best."

He handed me the eggs and I took them in both hands. I could feel their coolness evaporating in my sweaty palms. "Thanks," I said.

"I hope you will remember me when the batch is finished," he said, and his eyes became black beads in the wrinkles again.

"Well, nice meeting you."

"And nice to meet you, Josh."

When he shut the door behind me, I walked down the sidewalk toward my sister's apartment and then veered off and jogged back to Travis's. I pushed through his front door and held up the eggs.

"I told you he's a fat fuck, didn't I?" he said.

"He's big, yeah."

"See, that's why I need you in on this. I can't take him myself, if it comes to that. It's a two-man job and I figure you aren't gonna puss out on me or something. We'll split it fifty-fifty. It's an in-and-out deal. And then we can buy shit, you know. Get a car, do something more than sit here and fry all fucking summer." Travis had done a stint in juvie for a B and E, but since all he nabbed was a VCR, they gave him short time and sealed his record. He told me the best thing about being locked up was learning how to make pruno.

"Yeah, but how do you figure we're both gonna be in there and he isn't gonna recognize us? I mean, you're the fucking apartment manager and I was just in there borrowing eggs."

"Have another beer, Josh. This is one of those two-stage plans. Getting in is stage one, man."

I lost count at six beers, but I drank more beyond that before Travis staggered into the bedroom and called me to follow him. He turned on the light and lifted the corner of his mattress. His room smelled sweet, like overripe fruit. There were dirty clothes piled in the corners and dishes on the floor.

"Check this out, Josh."

He fished around under his mattress and I thought maybe this was where Travis showed me his porn collection and we busted a nut over some tits, but instead he pulled out a small gun and held it up to the light.

"What the hell," I said.

"I traded this guy a half-ounce of weed for this thing. Stupid fuck, huh? A .38 for a half. If it was me, I would've wanted the full ounce, but whatever. I tried it after I got it. Took it out to the dump one night with a flashlight and shot rats. Goddamn, you shoulda seen it. You hit those fuckers just right and they explode. Like a cantaloupe, man. This thing turned them inside out."

He twirled the trigger ring on his index finger and spun it until the butt was in his hand. He held it over his straight left arm and sighted down the barrel. "Bam bam bam," he said. "Almost

Clint Eastwood style, man. Here." He handed me the gun and I held it. I had never touched one before and it was heavier than I imagined, but in a solid way that made me understand how firing shots from it would be powerful, the kick vibrating all the way up to the shoulder. Then I realized why Travis was handing me the gun and I tossed it onto his unmade bed.

"I'm not killing anyone, Travis."

"Shhhhh. Listen to me, Josh." He leaned in close to me and I could see the wetness on his lips and smell the stale beer on his breath. He was slurring and his eyes were red. He squeezed my shoulder while he talked. "You don't have to kill him. And me, I ain't really killing him. He's a poor, fat bastard, Josh. He's gonna die. And it'll probably be soon. My father was a fat fuck like that and he finally just sat his ass on the recliner in the living room and drank himself right into a fucking grave, bad heart and all. And you know what, nobody cared when he died." He punctuated each word with a spray of spit that hit my cheek, but I was afraid to wipe it away, afraid to move. His hand squeezed tighter. "I didn't care at all. It was suicide. And that fat guy, no one visits him. No one ever comes over. I've been watching his apartment for weeks and weeks and it's just him and his sorry-ass bags of groceries. No one will care. Not you and not me, Josh. Not when we're counting our money and driving our cars." He let go of my arm and sat down on the bed. He pushed the gun around on the sheets. "We get one good shot at him and it's suicide. We leave a note. When the cops come around you can say what a nice guy he was, how you borrowed eggs from him one time. You can tear up a little at the sadness of it all."

"Travis, let's say this all goes off." In my head I didn't believe it would, and I wouldn't go through with it even if it were twenty thousand in that can and the most we'd do was kick him around the room a little, but I had to know how far Travis had planned, how much he thought about all the angles. "There are apartments all around us. It's summer. Open windows, people walking by. You think no one is gonna hear a gunshot and be out on their porch before we can even get his front door open?"

Travis smiled and wiped a hand across his mouth. He picked up a pillow from the bed and covered the end of the barrel. "He'd want it to be like this. He's a polite fat guy. No noise and not so much mess. It works. I tried it. Nothing more than a pop. Could be a backfire. Could be anything."

Travis leaned back on the bed and put the pillow over his face and shoved the gun against it. I could barely hear his voice. "Suicide. Good-bye, cruel world, and all that crap." He was still laughing when I left.

Travis picked up extra shifts at the Chevron station and I didn't see him for a while. I spent my evenings on the stairs to my sister's apartment, watching the traffic go by and listening to the occasional crowd noise from the Little League field across the street. I called home sometimes but no one answered. Sometimes I worried about my mom and Larry, but I didn't know if I would go back, even if she called me. As long as the checks kept coming, this was where I lived, free rent and Travis buying me beer.

I was sketching in my book when Percy walked by, a grocery bag in his arms. He stopped in front of the stairs and shifted the bag to his hip.

"Enjoying the evening, Josh?"

I closed my sketchbook and capped my pen. "It's nicer outside than sitting upstairs," I said.

"Nothing like the warmth to carry everything from cut grass

to steak in the air, is there?" He inhaled deeply and looked out at the street. "Would you like to come over for some dinner? I just picked up a few things and a bottle of decent wine. It'd be a shame to waste it all on myself."

My stomach made a low noise. I was living off of PBJs and Ramen, with the occasional boiled hot dog thrown in. My sister's cupboards were emptying and I hadn't seen her for a while.

"Are you sure you don't mind?" I asked. "I mean, I'd really appreciate it."

"Then it's a done deal."

I offered to carry his grocery bag, but he waved me away and I just had to follow behind him with my sketchbook tucked under my arm. I shot a quick look at Travis's apartment, and even though I knew he wasn't home, I felt guilty somehow.

Once inside Percy's apartment, he flicked on lights and opened the wine. I was used to the cheap beer Travis lifted from the Chevron, and the first drink from my glass made my throat close up and my eyes water.

"I prefer a muscular cabernet, but with Thai food I settle for a merlot. You like Thai food, Josh?"

I had never had Thai food and I wasn't sure what he meant by it. "Sure," I said. Anything sounded better than peanut butter.

"I think I'll make chicken in peanut sauce. A little noodle dish. It's my specialty," Percy said.

Peanut butter and noodles, I thought. I'd been eating Thai food for days and didn't even know it.

"Make yourself comfortable, Josh. Do you mind country music?"

I did, but I didn't say so.

"It's not really country, not in the true sense of the word. It's better than that. It's Dolly Parton, the best thing to happen to music since radio, if you ask me. No one really asks me, of course, but in my opinion an angel fell from heaven when she was born in Tennessee."

Percy pulled a record from a sleeve and set it on the turntable. I had seen records but never heard one play before. There was a scratchy sound and then a guitar took over and the hiss went away. Dolly's voice came from the speakers. Percy went into the kitchen and I flipped through the albums stacked in the milk crate on the shelf. They were all Dolly Parton records. Some of the covers were faded and several titles were repeated. There must have been sixty in the crate.

"My mother left them to me," Percy said. "They were my inheritance. My mother was an excellent cook and a well-intentioned woman, but she never really understood the complexities of the financial world. She thought that paying taxes was optional, like donating to charity. Needless to say, when all was said and done, it took most of my money and all of hers to put things back together again."

I sat in the living room while Percy cooked. He kept up a steady stream of conversation, and between his voice and the wine in my glass that never stood empty for more than a minute, I could've stretched out on his couch and fell asleep. Everything he talked about had a story behind it. There was never a simple sentence. By the time he set a plate of food in my hands, my head was buzzing.

He ate slowly and took small bites. I tried not to watch him, but the way his hands moved around his plate kept me hypnotized. His hands were delicate and slight, they looked almost soft, and the nails were long and rounded. I shoveled the food into my mouth without a breath.

"I haven't always been fat," Percy said. "I'm sure you can't imagine that, but it's true. Oh, I hated becoming fat. I fought against it, like one might do when drowning, I suppose, that same struggle of the body, but then I gave into it and there was peace. The very day that my mother died I went out and bought a Christmas ham. She used to make one every year, one of those with the thick, sticky glaze on it, all pink on the inside, marred only by the occasional white vein of fat. And I bought one at a store and I sat in my living room and I played the albums from that crate, in order, the early days to Dolly's present success, and I ate the ham slice by slice. And I was happy. There was no regret, no guilt, no fight of my body. I felt no illness afterward. Just this deep contentment. I can't explain it."

My fork scraped ceramic and my plate was empty. I hadn't realized my food was gone.

"Would you like more, Josh? There is plenty in the pan. Help yourself."

I wondered what it would be like to just keep eating, even though I could feel my stomach straining against the top of my jeans. I wondered what it would be like to keep going, break through that wall of being full and fight past my mind's urge to stop. "I can't eat another bite," I said.

Percy took my plate into the kitchen and brought back a bottle of wine. He set it on the coffee table in front of us and shook a cigarette out from a pack. "Do you mind if I smoke? I just love the flavor after a meal. It's the only time I indulge, which as you can imagine is quite often."

The record changed on the turntable and Percy leaned over to turn up the volume. "This is one of my favorites," he said.

Through the small opening in his window I could hear laughter and the sound of car doors slamming. I could hear televisions and the occasional sound of footsteps as someone walked by.

"Tell me about yourself, Josh. What do you do? Where do you come from?"

Percy filled my glass and handed it to me. He settled back in the couch and I could feel the weight shift in the cushions. The cigarette smoke clung to the air above us and dimmed the light.

"I like to draw," I said.

"Really. That's remarkable. Such a wonderful skill, really. Artistry. So few can visualize the world and then recreate it in its own likeness. I'd love to see your work, if you'd be willing."

"I'm not that good," I said. "It's a hobby."

"Oh, I'm sure there's more to it. Never be ashamed to have talent."

My face felt warm and I could feel the sweat on my palms. I rubbed my free hand on my jeans and emptied my glass in three swallows. Percy smiled at me. I handed him my sketchbook.

I watched him thumb through the pages. His eyes narrowed and his mouth tightened at the corners. Occasionally he smiled. I felt stupid and wanted to yank the sketchbook out of his hands and run out the door, but instead I poured more wine and I was so nervous that I had to chase the rim of the glass with the neck of the bottle so that they kissed off each other in a rattle that could be heard above the music. Percy didn't look up. I had sixty-three drawings in the sketchbook and he paused at every one of them.

By the time he closed the pad I had sweated through the armpits of my T-shirt and my spit was thick in my mouth. I didn't give a fuck about a fat guy looking at my drawings, but at the same time I couldn't convince my balls to come down from my stomach.

At last he exhaled deeply and picked another cigarette from the pack. After he shook the match out, he turned toward me and set the sketches on the table. "These are sensational, Josh. By that I don't mean that they're nice and you should hang them on your refrigerator with magnets. These show real promise. You have a gift."

"No one's ever told me that," I said. I let myself smile and everything loosened inside of me. "I mean, a teacher at school told me I did a good job, but . . ." My voice trailed off and broke up like the smoke above us.

"'Good' is an understatement."

There were no clocks in Percy's living room. When I thought I had run out of things to tell him, he pulled more from me, so that I told him everything—my mom and Larry, my sister gone, my father with his snowmobile dealership in North Dakota, how the one time he sent me a birthday card he'd signed it *Jim*. I told him things that Travis didn't know. The entire night, he never interrupted or changed the direction of the conversation. He just listened and drained me until I finally stood on shaky legs and told him I had to go home.

I had told him too much. I would've been less ashamed if I'd just bent over, gagged, and spilled my dinner onto his carpet. He handed me my sketchbook and walked me to the door. Outside the air was cool and there were crickets in the bushes. The traffic on the street had stopped. The rest of the apartments were dark and the only other sound was his door clicking shut behind me after he wished me a good night and gave me the open invitation to come back anytime.

I was wide awake and restless in my sister's apartment. I opened the windows to let in the breeze and I stripped down to my underwear in the darkness. In the bathroom I pulled my sister's *Jane* magazine out of the wicker rack by the toilet and thumbed to page 32: "The Cameron Diaz Interview." I pushed my underwear down to my ankles and sat on the closed seat. I started slow and closed my eyes for a second so I could see her in my head, her blond hair against my chest while I did her from behind and she watched me over her shoulder with that wicked look, just like in the picture. I was hard and breathing heavy when the magazine slid off the edge of the tub and folded facedown on the bathroom rug. I thought about leaving it that way and just going ahead, but I liked the way she smiled and I wanted to come to that picture. When I picked up the magazine the pages opened to a Calvin Klein ad and I held it there for a second. The guy was on his back with his arm cocked behind him—shirtless—with his jeans unbuttoned and opened in a V that ended just past the point that there should've been something more to see. He had long hair, like a girl, and his face was soft and open, his mouth full, and I wondered what it would be like to put my hand on his skin, how it would feel to touch that much hardness and muscle, how his mouth would look if it were on mine, and I kept looking at the ad while my left hand stroked in its familiar rise and fall. And I wondered what it would feel like to be next to Percy, all of his skin so loose and soft and his weight heavy like the sound of my breath in the bathroom, all of him around me, the Calvin Klein model hard in front of me, and me in the middle when I came.

I woke up to the sound of banging on my door and Travis yelling through the wood that if I wasn't dead, I'd better open the fuck up. I pulled on my jeans and unlocked the door. He was standing on the porch with two twelve-packs and a bag of Doritos. "Come on, man, it's supposed to hit a hundred fucking degrees today. We have to drink plenty of fluids."

We sat shirtless in lawn chairs in the shade of the awning and Travis pulled the garden hose around to the front of his apartment so we could spray ourselves. "Where the fuck were you last night, man? I came by to hang out but your place was dark, so I went to the bar."

I took a long drink of warm beer. "I was out. You know."

"I know, I know. You were out banging some chick and you don't want to talk about it. Whatever."

"Yeah, something like that."

"My time will come." He lifted his index finger above his head and swung his arm in a wide circle. "One of these days one of these chicks will come up short on the rent and then I'll take it in trade. It happens." A lawn mower started up across the street. "Your sister was never short on the rent. Too bad for me."

I took the hose and sprayed my chest with the water. Mrs. Santana opened her front door and one of her cats ran out and disappeared in the bushes under her window. "Now, she was short on her rent one time," Travis said. "But I let that shit slide."

We moved our lawn chairs with the shade and drank beer through the afternoon. "We haven't talked about the fat guy in a few days, Josh. I'm beginning to think you're gonna puss out on me."

I was quiet for a minute. I could feel Travis looking at me. "I didn't say I was pussing out. I just don't think it's a good thing to do."

"This ain't about good and bad, Josh. This is about right and wrong. It's right to help him out and help ourselves in the process. It's wrong that someone so fucked up should have what we don't."

"What makes you think he's so miserable?" I asked.

"I just know," Travis said. "Besides, Donny down at Chevron is selling a 'sixty-eight fastback Mustang and he'll unload it to me for under two grand. I'll take that son of a bitch and drop a 347 in it with Flowmasters and a Hurst shifter. Turn it into a competition piece.

"So I say we do it tonight. Me and you. The peak of summer and we'll have cash to burn. You go over there and get him to let you in, get him talking, sitting down. I sit in my place and wait for you to flick the lights on and off over there, and in I come. Done, and done."

"You're fucking crazy, Travis. It ain't even close to working. No way."

Travis pulled a beer out of the ice chest between us. "I think it'll work, or maybe you and your sister are problem tenants. I'd hate to see you have to go." He looked out across the courtyard at Percy's closed window.

"You can't do that. That's bullshit."

"Oh, I can and I will. I'll make sure you couldn't rent a Tuff Shed in this town. And then it'll get ugly, you know. Clint Eastwood style."

When it was dark outside I knocked on Percy's door. The courtyard was filled with the steady hum of air conditioners. The night was still and thick and it was hard to breathe. Travis was waiting for my signal, the flick of the lights, but if there was no signal, then he'd know something wasn't right and it wasn't gonna happen, and sometimes things don't happen, through no fault of my own. I had spent the early evening calling information for all of the James Reeds listed in Grafton and I thought maybe I had found the number for my father. Maybe he would send me a bus ticket. I could convince him it was temporary. A visit until I could disappear completely.

Percy answered the door and invited me in before I said hello. I could smell incense and bacon, both of them mixing together so that my stomach did a slow roll and I had to put my hand on it until it evened out again. I was shaking and there was sweat on my upper lip. I licked it away.

"Josh, it's such a pleasure. Please, sit down and make yourself at home." He gestured toward the couch and I shuffled over and fell into the cushions. The air conditioner kicked on and I could feel the vent blow the coolness across the room. I heard Percy in the kitchen behind me and the sound of dishes in the sink, the tap running, and then he was next to me, shifting his weight to sit.

"I've been thinking about you, Josh, about your art."

I didn't say anything. I knew that outside his window, in the apartment across the courtyard, Travis was sitting in his living room with a .38 in the waistband of his jeans.

"You know, I have many friends who could help you get established. I was talking about you to one of them, and he wanted to see your work. I told him I would talk to you. This is very exciting, Josh. This friend of mine is someone who could show you the right paths to take, who would take your work to the next level, on a grander scale. Take you out of the sketchbook, if you will, and put you on walls."

He reached forward and picked a narrow box up from the table. He handed it to me. "I saw these and I thought of you immediately."

I held the box in my hand and looked at him. "Go ahead. Open it," he said.

I pulled the wrapper off and opened the box. Inside were five pens, Rapidographs, the best. One pen cost almost thirty bucks. I'd seen them in magazines.

"You must have the right tools and the right environment. Everything must work toward the completion of your art."

I lifted one of the pens from the box and uncapped it. I touched my finger to the tip. The point was narrow and it pricked like a needle. The dot it left behind was so small I could barely see it. "These are amazing," I said.

"Josh, I think you have such a prospective future in front of you. I'm not sure you realize your potential. You see, Dolly never doubted her talent, knew it from the time she got her first guitar at the age of eight. She modeled herself after the town whore and was punished for wearing makeup, but how could anyone know what aspirations she had set in her mind, what with her eleven siblings fighting over every scrap of white trash? But there came a time for her, a turning point really, when she pushed her chair back from her plate of whistle pig and greens and packed a bag for Nashville. Porter Wagoner saw her talent and he snatched her up. It's a beautiful story.

"I want to snatch you up, Josh. I see your talent, your striking features and your eyes, all of your sensitivity. Porter and Dolly, Verlaine and Rimbaud. Percy and Josh." He was breathing heavy beside me.

His hand found mine on the couch beside him and he wrapped his fingers around it. I could feel the heat of his hand, the softness of his skin. It was all around me. The air conditioner kicked on again and the sound of his breath was buried beneath it. My heart struggled in my chest, like my ribs had closed in. I looked at the pens and thought about what a fine line they could draw.

"Josh?" he said.

I leaned toward the table, and with my free hand I reached for the lamp.

ROUNDING THIRD

Spark and me sobered up just inside the door to room 9 at the Sandpiper Motel. It was my seventeenth birthday and Spark had bought a bottle and a tank full of gas so he could drive me out to the lake and feed me fried chicken under the stars. On the way back he went left onto Highway 24 instead of right, and when I asked him if he realized what he'd done, he just smiled so that the dashboard lights lit up his face.

"I told you I had one more present," he said.

We had checked in under the name of Mr. and Mrs. Sting, since Spark had always been a diehard Police fan. "The Police," Spark would say, "not that shit Sting did when he left the band." My head was racing with Jim Beam and brown gravy, and by the time Spark got the key into the lock, I thought I'd be just as happy if we fell into bed and went to sleep instead.

The room was small with a double bed in the middle with a beat-up and bruised headboard against the wall. There was one nightstand and a lamp with a pull chain, and Spark fumbled it on while I kicked off my shoes and switched the six stations on the television. Everything on the channels was in black and white. There was a fan on the dresser, the kind that you could push the button on and the face of it moved slowly left and slowly right so that it didn't just blow air on one spot in the room. The carpet was green and thick, with dark stains, and there was a picture of a dock beneath a sunset on the wall.

Spark switched on the light in the bathroom and I could hear him lift the toilet lid to take a leak. "It smells good in here," he said. "Kind of like lemon."

I went into the bathroom and looked at my face in the mirror. The light made my skin look yellow, and I pinched at my cheeks with my fingers until the red surfaced again. There was a shine of chicken grease around my mouth, and I took a thin white washcloth off the rack and dabbed at my face with cold water until the shine had moved to my lips instead.

Spark hit the handle on the toilet and ran his hands under the faucet. He had been a waiter once and he was always careful about keeping his hands clean. He didn't last long as a waiter, though, not because he ignored the friendly sign that reminded the employees to wash before returning to work, but because Spark wasn't good with carrying so many plates at a time and remembering who ordered the pasta and who had the steak. He said waiting tables wasn't like carburetors or transmissions or a gutted Buick on the rack. A Buick never asked for another fork or an extra plate or dressing on the side.

"This is the best present I've ever had," I told him, and I leaned into him so I could stand on my tiptoes and kiss him on the cheek.

"Wait until after the next couple hours," he said, and he slapped me on my back jeans pocket.

I went into the room and turned back the bedspread. It was the kind with a design on top—this one had purple and orange flowers with bright green vines—and thin cotton lining underneath. It made an electric sound when I pulled it to the floor. The top sheet was white and cold and cuffed. There were two pillows, both of them thick and long. I slid between the sheets and propped myself up on the pillow. It was so firm that my chin tucked into my chest at an angle that made the back of my neck hurt. On the television, a woman in a gray dress was behind a wall and asking three men in gray shirts and black pants some questions. One of the men was smiling and nodding his head. I figured she would pick him, even though she couldn't tell that he had a big gap between his two front teeth.

"You coming to bed, Spark?" I yelled. It felt funny to say that, but I liked it a lot. Spark had stayed over at my house when my mom was out for the night, which was a lot, and we'd had sex in the backseat of his car before, but this was someplace new and neutral, someplace that didn't belong to either of us and for eighteen bucks tonight would be ours alone.

"Hold on, baby," Spark said from the bathroom. I could see his shadow moving on the open door. I heard the water running again, and then the light turned off and he was standing in the doorway in nothing but his underwear. "Happy birthday to you," he sang in a girly, breathy voice. "Happy birthday to you. Happy birthday, Mr. President." He dropped his hands to his knees and blew me a kiss.

"You're scaring me, Spark, come to bed."

"I was doing Marilyn," he said.

"If you come to bed right now, you can do her for real," I said.

"You better have your shirt off, Norma Jean."

I slid my T-shirt over my head and swung it around so that when I let go it hit the television and knocked the rabbit ears to the floor. The station went *shhhhh* with static. Spark hit the TV button and pulled the chain on the light, and then he was next to me and I could smell Ivory soap and wet hair.

The sheets pulled around us, and he was above me, breathing against my neck, and I was trying to hook my feet into the elastic of his underwear so that I could pull them down without having to use my hands. It was a trick I'd practiced but hadn't quite perfected, and sometimes I ended up binding his thighs together with my foot stuffed between his balls.

"What's that noise?" I said. It was coming from outside, something that started low and whined higher and higher until it fell off to low again.

"It's me, baby. It's my heart beating right here." Spark had my pants unhooked and was wriggling them down under the covers.

"No, listen, Spark. There it goes again." Spark stopped moving under the sheets and I could hear him breathing. "Hold your breath," I said. The room went silent except for the faucet dripping in the bathroom.

The whine came again, softer this time, but still that high cry that fell back and rose again. "There," I said. "That noise."

Spark lifted his head from the covers. "It's a cat," he said. "Some female cat in heat. I used to hear them all the time in the summer around my neighborhood. It used to freak me out, that sound, the way they sound like they're hurting so bad and all they really want is to get laid. It's fucking sad when you think about it." Spark went back to sliding my jeans down my legs and I stared up at the ceiling and thought about some stray cat outside, calling to anyone who would listen. The noise started up again.

"I can't take this, Spark. I can't concentrate with that noise out there."

Spark climbed back on top and I could feel his chest muscles moving against me. "Just block it out of your mind, Norma Jean. I mean, it's just a cat who wants what we're getting right here. It's not so different from us." I could feel him move forward, my cue to open my legs and let him in, but the noise was building again and I put my knees down.

"I can't," I said.

Spark rolled off and pushed his bangs back with the heel of his hand. He exhaled hard. "Norma Jean, honey, it's your birthday. You want me to turn the television back to a game show and you can come to someone winning a new car instead? Would that make it better?"

"I just don't like that noise."

"You know, my friend Victor back in the neighborhood once told me that you can get a cat out of heat if you stick something inside it—you know, like a thermometer or something. Something that makes it think it's getting fucked, when actually it's not."

"That is sick, Spark, really sick. Please don't tell me you ever did that."

"Me? No way. I wasn't a big cat fucker back in my day, but Victor, I don't know. He said it worked."

"I just want the noise to stop."

"Honey, I'm not walking out there with my car keys or a Q-Tip or something and fucking the cat just so me and you can get back to what we came here to do. So you tell me what else I can do to make you lie back down and make some of those noises of your own." Spark bit at his lip and pulled the sheet up over his waist.

"Maybe if I turn on the shower I won't hear the noise."

"Perfect. It'll be like a waterfall in the background. We can pretend we're camping and whatever cat noise filters through can just be some mountain lion coming up to our fire circle to lick the scraps."

I got out of bed and went into the bathroom. In the light through the curtains I could see the sink and the toilet, the bathtub against the wall. I felt around the inside of the tub until I found the faucet and I turned the hot and cold on halfway.

"I already smell pine needles," Spark yelled from the bed.

I reached for the handle to turn on the water to the shower, and all I felt was faucet and taps. "Spark, I can't find the shower thing," I yelled.

Spark turned on the light and I had to cover my eyes for a second before I could see again. "You could've warned me," I said.

"Look, if we don't get the waterfall going and get back to bed in the next thirty seconds, we're gonna have to start all over again." He looked down at his waist.

"There's no shower," I said.

We both looked at the wall and saw only white plaster where a showerhead should've been. The mirror was fogging up. "Okay, it's okay," he said. "It's a river, class five rapids, and we're rafting them tomorrow—this might be our last chance to fuck. We could drown in the morning. Get back to the sleeping bag and let's—"

"It won't work, Spark," I said. I turned the taps until the water cut off. The room was suddenly quiet.

Spark leaned back against the sink and I could see that our thirty seconds had passed. "You wanna watch TV?" he said. "We still have another bottle and three pieces of chicken in the car."

I felt like I was going to cry. My throat was tight and I could feel my eyes filling. I turned my head so Spark couldn't see me. The noise came again. From this side of the building we could tell it was coming from the back side of the motel, somewhere along the walls. Spark walked over to the window and slid it up so he could see out the screen. He cupped his hands around his face to block out the glare. "Here, kitty kitty kitty," he called. "Come here, you little son of a bitch."

"Do you see anything?" I asked. I wiped my eyes on the back of my hand.

"Nothing but trash. No cats." The noise came again, loud this time, like the cat was right under our window.

"Jesus," I yelled. "That was loud. It has to be right there." I stood up next to Spark and looked out at the night. There was a hillside behind the motel, a sandy slope with scrub weeds that smelled like star thistle. In the light from the parking lot I could see the wink of cans and something that looked like a milk carton.

"Kitty kitty kitty."

"Maybe it's hurt," I said. "Maybe something attacked it. Maybe one of those tractor trailers on the highway rolled it under its tires and it's bleeding to death right under our window. You gotta go out there and see, Spark. Please."

"I really don't think it's a smart thing for me to go out behind a highway motel in search of a stray cat that may or may not be wild and may or may not be torn up. I've been scratched by a cat before and that shit hurts."

"Maybe you'll scare it away at least. And then that noise will be gone and we can get back in bed and maybe it can be like that time at the movies when I was sitting next to you and I told you to move the popcorn. Remember?"

"You'd do that?"

"I'd love to do that again."

"But I thought you wouldn't, you know . . . the whole way. Because it made you gag."

"I'll let you. I promise."

Spark went back in the other room and I could hear the bed-spread fabric rustling and his zipper going up. "You stay by the window in case I need help," Spark said. I heard the door shut and there was silence again. A truck went by on the highway and the window shook a little and then was still.

"Kitty kitty kitty," I called. A cricket started playing somewhere in the weeds on the sand. Another cricket answered. I turned off the bathroom light so I could see outside better. We were in the second-to-last room at the end of the complex, and I heard Spark's shoes as he turned the corner. There was the crunch of gravel, and then the quiet of sand.

"Norma Jean?" he whispered. "You still there?"

"You see anything yet?"

"Nothing. Which window are you at? They all look the same."

"Right here." I scratched my nails up and down the screen so that it made a metallic sound.

"It smells like piss back here."

"Just be careful."

Spark started calling for the kitty again and I pushed my head against the screen as hard as I could so that I could see in both directions. Not one shadow moved. Spark was kicking at the garbage.

"It has to be gone," he said. He kept kicking around. I heard cans rolling against bottles. "There's some blankets back here," he said. "A bundle of them under the window next door." I heard him walk past the window and the sound of more cans knocking around and then the cry again, softer this time, but close.

"Son of a bitch," Spark said. His voice sounded pale.

"What is it, Spark? Is it hurt? Don't touch it if it's wild."

"You ain't gonna believe this," he said, and then I heard him running and his shadow moved past the window so quickly that for a second I lost my breath. I could hear my pulse in my ears.

Spark slammed through the front door and shut it behind him. "Turn on the lights, Norma Jean, this is bad bad bad." He had a bundle in his hands and he laid it on the bed while I went for the lights. All I could think was that I hoped there wasn't blood. I couldn't stand the sight of blood, especially if there was a cut involved or any kind of wound. I turned on the lights and kept my hand ready to cover my eyes.

Spark lifted the blanket back and I had to lean in closer to make sure I was seeing right. There was a baby in the blankets, its hands balled next to its cheeks, and it was very much alive.

"Son of a bitch," I said. I moved in closer and reached my hand out to touch it and then pulled it back again. "What the hell, Spark. What the hell is this?"

Spark had both his hands shoved deep in his pockets. He was shifting his weight back and forth on his feet like he had to pee suddenly. "Uncover it," he said. "We gotta check it, I think. See if it has some ID or something."

"Oh sure, Spark, where would that be? In its wallet?"

"I don't know. Shit. Maybe it has a note or a bracelet or something."

"I don't think someone would leave a note on a baby they dumped behind a motel."

"Just unwrap it," Spark said.

"Why me?"

"You're a woman. This is a baby. This is totally your thing."

"My thing? This isn't my baby."

"Yeah, but it's supposed to come natural and all. All women are mothers and stuff."

I reached forward and pulled the blanket loose around the baby. Its eyes were squeezed shut and there was a small scratch on its cheek. "Shhhhh," I said as I bent toward it.

"See, that's good. You're doing great," Spark said.

"I haven't done anything."

"Yeah, but you're making that sound. That's a good sound. I never would've thought of that."

Under the blanket, the baby was wrapped in a white T-shirt. Its legs were pulled tight against its stomach, and I carefully unwrapped it from the folds of cloth. It opened its mouth but no sound came out.

I lifted the T-shirt and saw the bare skin, the purple blotches scattered all over. It had a penis. "Boy," I said.

"Poor guy." Spark dropped his hands to his crotch and clasped them together.

"His skin is still warm. Look," I said. I pointed at the belly button. There was a thing that looked like a dark vine sticking out about three inches. "It's the cord." I lifted the baby up to me and he startled. I started rocking him back and forth. "Pull the blanket off our bed, Spark," I said. "And get one of those big towels out of the bathroom."

Spark brought me the towel and I wrapped the baby in it as best I could. He wasn't very big. Once he was tight in the towel, I wrapped the blanket from our bed all around him and set him in my lap. The bundle was fifty times bigger than the baby. I put my finger to his lips and he started sucking at it, turning his head to find it when I pulled it away. "He's gotta eat," I said.

"So feed him," Spark said.

"Feed him what, Spark? Chicken and Jim Beam?"

"I don't know. Jesus. Can't you breast-feed him or something? I mean, that's why you got 'em, right?"

"I don't have milk, Spark. You have to actually have a baby in order to get the rest of the stuff, okay? We need a bottle. And some juice. No, milk. Shit, I don't know. I can't remember if Jeanie put milk in Leah's bottle or formula. I think it was in a can."

"Don't they need special food?"

"Okay, formula. You gotta go find some formula, Spark. Right now."

"Can you just get that at a store? Or do you need a prescription or something?"

"At the store, Spark. Jesus. Just drive up the highway and find something that's open. And get some diapers."

Spark picked up his car keys and turned toward the door. "Wait a minute," he said. "Why are you doing all this? It's two in the morning and we've got an abandoned baby in a motel. All I need is a phone and I can call the cops and have them come out here and take over."

"Yeah, Spark, they'd love to take over, especially when you're almost twenty years old with a girl who just turned seventeen in a motel by the highway. Are you forgetting about that?"

"Shit," Spark said. He leaned back against the closed motel door and knocked his head back and forth against the emergency evacuation card.

"Not only that, but you know what they'll do with him? They'll put him in the system. He'll end up in a foster home. You know what happens there."

"Maybe they can find his mom."

"Oh yeah, sure, Spark. She dumps her baby out a motel window and she's just down at the Denny's having pancakes. She's long gone. She's probably on a Greyhound headed east by now."

"I was in a foster home when my dad was in and out of jail that time. I did okay."

"Spark, you lived with your grandma."

"I know, but it was hard. She made me eat eggs every day for breakfast."

"Just go find a store and get the formula, a bottle, and some diapers, okay? It's the least we can do. He's starving."

Spark opened the door and a minute later I heard the car start. I kept rocking the baby in my lap and promising him that nothing bad would happen. We'd take care of him. By the time Spark came back with the grocery bag, I was convinced that the picture on the wall was not a dock at sunset, but actually at sunrise, and somewhere in the bushes there were birds that I could hear but could not quite see.

The baby drank the first few ounces fast, and when I set him up to get a better grip on the bottle, the formula came right back up. "Oh, Jesus, he's sick," Spark said. "He'll probably die and then I'll go to jail just like my dad. Murder."

"Your dad went to jail for possession, Spark, not murder. He had a quarter pound of weed in his trunk."

"Yeah, but it killed my mom."

"He's just eating too fast. He's not used to it, I think." I tilted the bottle up and he sucked at the nipple so hard that I was afraid he'd pull it out, but then his lips slowed and I could see his cheeks relax each time he swallowed. He brought his fisted hands up to the bottle. When I thought he was asleep, I held him up against me and patted his back until he burped, and then I put him on his side to sleep. I lay down next to him. Outside, the darkness was draining out of the sky.

"You love me, don't you, Spark?" I asked.

"Of course I do."

"I mean, marrying love?"

"Someday I want us to get married."

"And we'll have a family, won't we?"

"You bet. All kinds of little Sparks and Norma Jeans running around the yard. Hell, I even want to get a dog. One of those bird dogs that get all stiff when they're out hunting."

"When do you think that'll happen, Spark?"

Spark leaned back on the bed and put his elbows behind his head. "I figure you'll be old enough to fuck without a felony next year, so you know, someday."

I swung my elbow backward and hit him in the ribs. "Hey," he said. "I was kidding."

"I'm not. This is serious."

Spark rolled onto his side and laid his arm across me so that he could hold me and the baby together. The baby made small noises in his sleep. "I'd like to think that I could get enough money and get us a place and we could get married soon," he said.

"Maybe we should take off and move away. Me and you and the baby. Start our family now, Spark. Like this. Don't you think it's meant to be? Finding a baby on my birthday? We can't ignore this."

"I don't think it could be that easy, Norma Jean honey. It ain't our baby. What're we gonna do, just drive into town with a baby and yell 'Surprise!'?"

"I don't want to go back to town. I want to get on the highway and go south. We could live on the ocean. You could go fishing, like you always wanted to do."

"And you could drive a convertible and maybe I'll make a movie," Spark said. "We don't have any money, Norma Jean. I could barely afford that can of formula and those diapers. I ain't ready to be a dad all the time and take care of a family. Someday, yeah, but right now, I don't think so."

"You said you could fix anything on four wheels, right?"

"Sure."

"Places always need mechanics, Spark. It doesn't matter where we live, you can get a job and I'll get a job and we'll just do it. We can make it."

Spark was quiet for a while. I thought maybe he was sleeping. "Spark?" I said. "This is what I always wanted with you."

"Me, too," he said finally.

"When it gets lighter out, I want you to go back to town and quit your job. Get Rudy to give you your last paycheck in cash. Tell him something came up. Then I want you to come back here and we'll head south, okay? The three of us."

"What about your stuff? Your clothes. What about your mom?"

I would miss some of the things in my room, and the new shorts I'd just bought two days ago. "It can all be replaced," I said.

I woke Spark when the sun was high in the window. The bed was warm and we were all covered in a light layer of sweat. I unwrapped the baby a little, changed his diaper. Spark had bought toddler diapers and I practically had to wrap the top of one around his little waist twice in order to tape it. I poured some more formula into the bottle. He drank it without opening his eyes. I wondered what color his eyes were, if they were blue or brown. He had a small wisp of dark hair that fell forward on his head like Spark's. I took a warm washcloth and gave him a sponge bath on the bed in the sun.

Spark showered and left. He promised to be back as soon as they processed his payroll and paid him out cash. He hoped that Rudy wouldn't make a big deal out of him quitting on the spot and not let him pack up his tools, but I didn't think Rudy was like that. I slept with the baby against me, watched television and waited. We were supposed to be out of the motel by five P.M., and I figured we'd be on the road by then.

While the baby slept, I got dressed and walked to the edge

of the parking lot. There was a pay phone near the office, and I went inside it and shut the door around me to drown out the sound of the cars on the highway. It was hot inside and smelled funny, like spoiled spilled beer. I turned myself so I could see the door to our room.

I was half-expecting that she wouldn't answer, that this was one of the nights when she didn't make it home, but she picked up on the third ring and hesitated before accepting the collect call.

"Hi, Mom," I said.

I heard her exhale cigarette against the receiver. "Don't 'Hi, Mom' me. Where are you?"

"Look, I just wanted to tell you that I'm going away for a little while, okay? But I'm fine. I'm okay."

"Don't play this with me, Norma Jean. If you did something, it can be fixed, but don't call here looking for some sympathy."

"I have to go, Mom. I'll send you a postcard."

"Don't ask me for any money, because I won't send it to you."

"I'll talk to you soon."

She was still talking when I hung up the phone.

Me and the baby watched game shows, and then a few soap operas came on. I could never keep any of the people straight. I found a movie on Channel 7, and I fed him again, changed his diaper. He didn't really cry much. If this was what it was like to be a mother, then I don't know why so many women bitched so much about taking care of a baby. All they did was eat and sleep and need a clean diaper every now and then.

When the movie was over, I started worrying about Spark. The light was changing outside, and even though there wasn't a clock, I could tell that it was deep afternoon. I stood at the curtains and looked out every time a car went by. I counted red cars.

When I got to thirty-eight, it pulled into the driveway and came to a stop in front of our room. I opened the door for Spark.

He hugged me tight and I could smell cigarette on him. "I sure did miss you," he said. He staggered a little bit and walked over to the bed. "How's Junior?"

"He's fine, Spark. Where in the hell have you been? I was worried."

Spark held up his hand toward me. "Okay, okay, it took a while. But I'm back and I got my tools and we can hit the highway."

"Are you drunk?"

"Nah. I ain't drunk. Jesus, what is this, an investigation?"

I walked over to him and leaned down. "You smell like booze and cigarettes."

He reached out and took my hand in his. "It's nothing," he said. There was blue stuff on his hand.

"What the hell is that?" I said.

He held his hand up to his face and squinted at it. "Chalk dust."

"You were shooting pool?" I could feel my stomach tighten, but I swallowed hard and the fist loosened in my gut.

"The guys wanted to take me out. I mean, shit, I'm leaving town. I'm moving away. It was a going-away party."

"You didn't tell them anything, did you?"

"I told them I got a better job. Somewhere." He started laughing and leaned back on the bed. His elbow landed on the baby, who he jerked and started crying. "Whoa, sorry there, Junior." Spark rocked the baby back and forth on the bed with his hand until the crying stopped. "I told them I had a good job waiting for me. I just didn't know where. They thought that was funny as shit."

"You got your tools okay?"

"Hell, Rudy even bought me a beer."

"And your paycheck. You got your money?"

"It's all right here." He rolled back on the bed and pulled his pants pockets inside out. Wadded-up ones, fives, and tens fell onto the bed. I picked them up and smoothed them out one by one. I counted the money, and then counted it again.

"There's forty-seven dollars here, Spark. Where's the rest of your paycheck? You shoulda been getting paid for close to two weeks. Where is it?"

"I told you, we had a small celebration. On account of me going away." He had his eyes closed and his voice was quiet. "And maybe I played a little pool. I thought maybe I could double our money. Get us started off right, you know?"

I folded the money and set it on the dresser. The five o'clock news was on TV. There was a fire in an apartment building. The weather would hit record highs by the end of the workweek. I sat on the edge of the bed and found my purse on the floor. There was footage of the Giants' game from the night before. The runner rounded third. Spark was snoring on the bed. He had one arm over the baby. The baby had his thumb in his mouth. I found my lipstick and put it on without a mirror. I combed out my hair and flattened it with my hand. Spark made a noise in his sleep and I wanted to marry him more than ever. I kissed the baby on the cheek so that my lipstick left behind a mark. He was panting fast like a puppy. I turned on the fan and hit the button so the face would move from left to right and the air would reach both of them.

The office was cool inside and the television on the back table was color. I could hear an air conditioner kick on and I turned toward the vent so I could lift my shirt a little and fan the cool air across my chest. I could smell bacon coming from a room I could not see. My stomach growled. I hadn't had anything to eat since the fried chicken under the stars and I felt paper thin, like I could fold myself up and slide back under the door behind me. I hit the tarnished brass bell on the counter. It made a dull ring that didn't seem to travel far enough to be of any use.

I heard a pan rattle and then a bead curtain parted and a man stepped up to the chipped counter. He was wearing a dirty T-shirt with holes under the armpits, and there were small bits of something caught in his mustache. His stomach swelled under his shirt and hung over the waistband of his shorts.

"Help you?" he said.

"I'm staying in number nine, down that way." I cocked my head to the right to emphasize the direction of the room, but his eyes didn't follow mine out to the parking lot. I cleared my throat. "We checked in last night."

He turned and looked at the clock on the wall. The minute hand was knocking against the seven. It was 5:35.

"Looks like you're checking in another night."

"You see, that's the problem. I didn't realize it was so late, and uh, my boyfriend isn't feeling well. I was wondering if we could stay a little longer."

"You bet," he said. I exhaled with relief and wiped at the sweat on my upper lip. "For eighteen more dollars, you can stay all night." He rested both hands on the counter and folded them together. His nails were clipped short and his hands were clean.

"I don't have eighteen more dollars," I said. I thought about the money on the dresser and the fact that there were only a few ounces of formula left in the can in the ice bucket on the nightstand.

"Well, that's a problem," he said. He lifted the edge of the sign-in book and ruffled the pages with his thumb. "I have a daughter about your age. She lives with her mother in Portland. I really miss her sometimes."

"Look, maybe I can clean some rooms for you, do some extra work. My boyfriend is really good at fixing cars, doing tune-ups. We'll do anything if you let us stay out the week until we can figure out how to get some money together."

He scratched his head and looked at his fingernails. He bit at whatever came away. "I already pay someone to clean rooms. And I don't need a mechanic. What else you got?"

I went through our possessions in my head. Spark had a cheap watch and I didn't have anything at all, not even a ring. "What about a car stereo?" I said.

"I don't have a car."

"Please, mister, we need the room for the rest of the week. What will it take?" I was biting at the inside of my cheek to keep from crying. He reached out and pinched the sides of my face together so that my mouth opened.

"Cover your teeth with your lips," he said. I pulled my lips over my teeth while he squeezed my cheeks together, his thumb on one side, his fingers on the other. He bobbed my head up and down. "That looks like thirty-six dollars," he said.

For ten minutes I could buy us two days. I thought about Spark and the baby curled up on the bed, both of them with their knees pressed against their chests. We were at the ball game and I was coming back with popcorn. It was the seventh-inning stretch and Spark and the baby were wearing matching Giants hats. I could see them in the bleachers behind the left-field fence. The man lifted the hinged end of the counter and I followed him through the beaded curtain toward the back of the office, and the room that smelled like bacon.